SWEET BIRD OF YOUTH

BY TENNESSEE WILLIAMS

PLAYS

Baby Doll & Tiger Tail

Camino Real (with Ten Blocks on the Camino Real)

Candles to the Sun

Cat on a Hot Tin Roof

Clothes for a Summer Hotel

Fugitive Kind

A House Not Meant to Stand

The Glass Menagerie

A Lovely Sunday for Creve Coeur

Mister Paradise and Other One-Act Plays:
These Are the Stairs You Got to Watch, Mister Paradise, The Palooka, Escape, Why Do You Smoke So Much, Lily?, Summer At The Lake, The Big Game, The Pink Bedroom, The Fat Man's Wife, Thank You, Kind Spirit, The Municipal Abattoir, Adam and Eve on a Ferry, And Tell Sad Stories of The Deaths of Queens . . .

Not About Nightingales

The Notebook of Trigorin

Something Cloudy, Something Clear

Spring Storm

Stairs to the Roof

Stopped Rocking and Other Screen Plays:
All Gaul is Divided, The Loss of a Teardrop Diamond, One Arm, Stopped Rocking

A Streetcar Named Desire

Sweet Bird of Youth (with The Enemy: Time)

The Traveling Companion and Other Plays:
The Chalky White Substance, The Day on Which a Man Dies, A Cavalier for Milady, The Pronoun 'I', The Remarkable Rooming-House of Mme. LeMonde, Kirche KWill Mr. Merriwether Return from Memphis?, The Traveling Companion

27 Wagons Full of Cotton and Other Plays:
27 Wagons Full of Cotton, The Purification, The Lady of Larkspur Lotion, The Last of My Solid Gold Watches, Portrait of a Madonna, Auto-Da-Fé, Lord Byron's Love Letter, The Strangest Kind of Romance, The Long Goodbye, Hello From Bertha, This Property is Condemned, Talk to Me Like the Rain and Let Me Listen, Something Unspoken

The Two-Character Play

Vieux Carré

THE THEATRE OF TENNESSEE WILLIAMS

The Theatre of Tennessee Williams, Volume I:
Battle of Angels, A Streetcar Named Desire, The Glass Menagerie

The Theatre of Tennessee Williams, Volume II:
The Eccentricities of a Nightingale, Summer and Smoke, The Rose Tattoo, Camino Real

The Theatre of Tennessee Williams, Volume III:
Cat on a Hot Tin Roof, Orpheus Descending, Suddenly Last Summer

The Theatre of Tennessee Williams, Volume IV:
Sweet Bird of Youth, Period of Adjustment, The Night of the Iguana

The Theatre of Tennessee Williams, Volume V:
The Milk Train Doesn't Stop Here Anymore, Kingdom of Earth (The Seven Descents of Myrtle), Small Craft Warnings, The Two-Character Play

The Theatre of Tennessee Williams, Volume VI:
27 Wagons Full of Cotton and Other Short Plays
includes all the plays from the individual volume of *27 Wagons Full of Cotton and Other Plays plus The Unsatisfactory Supper, Steps Must be Gentle, The Demolition Downtown*

The Theatre of Tennessee Williams, Volume VII:
In the Bar of a Tokyo Hotel and Other Plays
In the Bar of a Tokyo Hotel, I Rise in Flames, Cried the Phoenix The Mutilated, I Can't Imagine Tomorrow, Confessional The Frosted Glass Coffin, The Gn%odiges Fr%oulein, A Perfect Analysis Given by a Parrot, Lifeboat Drill, Now the Cats with Jeweled Claws, This is the Peaceable Kingdom

The Theatre of Tennessee Williams, Volume VIII:
Vieux Carré, A Lovely Sunday for Creve Coeur, Clothes for a Summer Hotel, The Red Devil Battery Sign

POETRY

Collected Poems

In the Winter of Cities

PROSE

Collected Stories

Hard Candy and Other Stories

One Arm and Other Stories

Memoirs

The Roman Spring of Mrs. Stone

The Selected Letters of Tennessee Williams, Volume I

The Selected Letters of Tennessee Williams, Volume II

Where I Live: Selected Essays

A painting of the New York stage setting for *Sweet Bird of Youth* by Jo Mielziner.

SWEET BIRD OF YOUTH

TENNESSEE WILLIAMS

INTRODUCTION BY LANFORD WILSON

A NEW DIRECTIONS BOOK

The publisher is grateful to Jo Mielziner for permission to reproduce his drawing of the stage set of the New York production, Copyright © 1959 by Jo Mielziner. The "Foreword" originally appeared in a slightly different form in *The New York Times* in 1959. *The Enemy: Time* was first published in the March 1959 issue of the magazine *The Theatre*.

Cover design by John Gall.
Front matter design by Rodrigo Corral Design.
Manufactured in the United States of America.
New Directions Books are printed on acid-free paper.
First published clothbound by New Directions in 1959.
First published as New Directions Paperbook 409 in 1975.
Reissued as New Directions Paperbook 1123 in 2008.
Published simultaneously in Canada by Penguin Canada Books, Ltd.

Library of Congress Cataloging-in-Publication Data:

Williams, Tennessee, 1911–1983.
Sweet bird of youth / by Tennessee Williams ; with an introduction by Lanford Wilson.–Revised ed.
p. cm.
"A New Directions book."
ISBN 978-0-8112-1807-8 (pbk. : acid-free paper)
1. Motion picture actors and actresses–Drama. 2. Saint Cloud (Fla.)–Drama. I. Title.
PS3545.I5365S87 2008
812'.54–dc22 2008027106

NEW DIRECTIONS BOOKS ARE PUBLISHED FOR JAMES LAUGHLIN
BY NEW DIRECTIONS PUBLISHING CORPORATION
80 EIGHTH AVENUE, NEW YORK 10011

CONTENTS

INTRODUCTION: THE PLEASANT DISGUISE OF ILLUSION

Tennessee Williams had the strongest work ethic of any writer I've known. As he said, he *had* to write. At his Key West home he would rise (very early I'm told–well, 6:00 a.m.), do a few laps in his pool, retire to his writing shack and sometimes not be seen again until after four or five in the evening. Seven days. I'm going on the word of his friends about the early rising, when I visited I never got to his place before noon. By 7:00 p.m. we'd watch the news–we were both Walter Cronkite fans. He would applaud the stock market report if stocks had fallen that day, "I own stock myself, but I get a kick when the market's down." For some reason I do too, always have, but I couldn't tell you why.

I was in Key West in 1971 to talk about *The Migrants*, a film for TV. The director, Tom Gries, had just finished shooting *The Glass House*, a television movie about prisons which had originally been written by Truman Capote, but was completely rewritten by someone else. Now Gries wanted to film a story about migrant farm workers, pickers–following the crops as they ripen, from Florida for celery and tomatoes in February, working up the coast with the seasons, ending in October, digging potatoes on Long Island. Following the precedent of his earlier project, Gries decided that Tennessee would be the perfect person for the subject and asked him if he were to write such a story, whom would he want to adapt it? I had just finished the libretto for Lee Hoiby's opera of *Summer and Smoke* and the three of us had a very successful relationship on that project, so a puzzled Tennessee said, "I don't know exactly what you're talking about." But he finally decided that I was just the right person to adapt something that had never been written. Later he also said, "I don't think I've sold *just* my name before, Lanford, but I don't think they're paying me enough for it." We finally got down to thinking about the project and kicking over possible story lines, flying in a two-passenger plane (those damn things are kites and I hate to fly–fortunately Tennessee had brought a thermos of what turned out to be gin martinis) up to . . . I can't remember the name of the town. Sitting in a Florida Aid to Migratory Workers office we interviewed a migrant family and, with some of Tom Gries' ideas, came up with a plausible story. The billing on the piece was finally decided as: "from a story by Tennessee Williams, teleplay by Lanford Wilson." For the Emmys it had to be entered in the "Original Teleplay" category because there was never a published story from which it could have been adapted.

We talked about a lot of things–well, he talked, I listened. Tennessee had been everywhere, of course, and knew everyone, and I knew no one and hadn't been anywhere. It bored him to talk about his work, his plays, which was frustrating as hell for me, of course: a young writer would naturally like to absolutely grill the man, but beyond saying his favorite of his work was *Cat on a Hot Tin Roof*, and me saying mine was *The Night of the Iguana*, we didn't go near it. I (damn it, damn it) honored his reluctance. Now, of course, I wish to hell I had asked him about *Sweet Bird of Youth*.

I thought writing a few comments on this play was going to be easy. I had seen the 1959 national touring company in Chicago–I thought it was wonderful, but years later all I can remember is Kazan's direction of the opening moment. I'm pretty sure I read *Sweet Bird* in an earlier version published in *Esquire* prior to the Broadway opening, and certainly saw the Richard Brooks film a few years later. The first time I reread it, last month–the first contact I had had with it in nearly forty years–I was surprised at how simple, straightforward, bare and frankly melodramatic it was. I hadn't intended to read *Sweet Bird* again that day, I was just trying to find a particular passage, couldn't locate it anywhere in the first act, and ended up rereading the whole play. In the two hours that elapsed between readings someone had had their way with the script. For one simple example, I had been certain the word "castrate" was not in the play and thought it annoyingly coy, uncharacteristically prim, and unlike Tennessee not to be more straightforward. There it was, of course, bold as day, and in the first scene on about page twelve. But beyond that, the play had changed completely. It was not possible to ignore it. It said, "dismiss me at your peril." Whole scenes had fallen away, were not in the play at all. New scenes had obviously been added: I pride myself on a good memory and had no memory of them at all. Scenes that had seemed thin and tediously obvious were crowded with shadows, shadings and double meanings; speeches that had seemed self-indulgent, turgid even, were painfully revealing. I had thought Tennessee had aimed for "tragic" and ended up hitting melodrama square between the eyes. I was blind.

It is interesting to compare Tennessee's final 1959 play with the earlier one-act version from 1952, *The Enemy: Time* (published in this volume) and realize that the loss of youthful beauty and innocence was his theme from the beginning. Tennessee developed the character of Heavenly, and the tragic story of her trip to join Chance, and the dynamic Princess Kosmonopolis–another of the hugely impressive women's roles for which he is famous, and probably the most fun of the lot to play–the whole Boss Finley family, or gang, as well as Aunt Nonnie, The Heckler, Boss Finley's mistress and a slew of others. All this had been added, their stories developed over the seven years he worked on it, enlarging the play's length about fifteen times, and still the theme remains: the tragic loss of youthful beauty and innocence when that's all one has to offer.

Sweet Bird of Youth is not a realistic, naturalistic play, of course. None of Williams' work comes anywhere near the kitchen sink, and ambient sounds float through all of his work, from the bluesy piano melodies drifting up from the alley in *The Glass Menagerie* to the squeal of the no-neck monsters playing in the yard downstairs in *Cat*, but when you read *Sweet Bird* be especially sensitive to the play as he's written it, as he saw and heard it in his imagination. The frank stage light focused on a single character as he comes stage front to tell his life story–Tennessee knows this is unconventional and he's saying, essentially, "I'm not going to go through all the realistic nonsense to work this into the play. Here is what you need to know." I don't believe anywhere in his work has he written a line as bald as the Princess's line to Chance: "That's a good way to begin to tell your life story. Tell me your life story." And by damn Chance does, out on the forestage, facing the audience, with the lights dimmed on everything else–for six pages. Be aware of the presentational quality of the play, and of the drifting, impressionistic lighting and sound. This is not realism. This is a dream that keeps going wrong.

I've always considered Tennessee as one of the main influences on the sexual revolution of the Sixties. He said he "slept through the Sixties" but whether or not that was true, he helped pave the way with the frank public airings about sensuality and sexuality provoked by his major plays. (Theater is a public forum, quite different from the privacy of a novel–you can read all sorts of sex in a book, but when it's blurted out from the stage, and you're helplessly sitting next to a stranger, buddy, it's out there!) I'm not talking about the sweetness and light of flower children or Woodstock–music remained rather prim for a while yet–I'm talking about the raw candor of the 1970s and '80s. In the early 1980s I participated in a forum on theater that degenerated, or perhaps lifted, to talking about the responsibility of the playwright, about human behavior, about the way we talk to one another, treat one another–the subject and language of that forum could not have happened before Tennessee allowed, demanded, that the truth about what and who we are be discussed openly. Even I was shocked at some of the twists the discussion took and some of the things I was saying. At the end the moderator said it was the most truthful and forthright forum he had ever witnessed and the audience stood, applauding.

But at the same time, just look at the quite fun but bowdlerized film of this play to see what was acceptable to a movie audience in 1962–Heavenly does not have a venereal disease in the film, she has an abortion; Chance is not subjected to castration, they break his nose! Good grief! If anything, Paul Newman would look even more interesting with a broken nose. At the end, of course, Heavenly and Chance leave a cloud of dust, happily speeding out of town, together at last, in her convertible. Bullshit! You could never turn to Hollywood for truth.

In *The Glass Menagerie,* Tennessee's most autobiographical play, the narrator Tom says, "I am the opposite of a stage magician. He gives you illusion that has the appearance of truth. I give you truth in the pleasant disguise of illusion." Return to this play, to the text. Tennessee (Tom) is still giving it.

LANFORD WILSON
JULY 2008
SAG HARBOR, NY

FOREWORD
By Tennessee Williams

When I came to my writing desk on a recent morning, I found lying on my desk top an unmailed letter that I had written. I began reading it and found this sentence: "We are all civilized people, which means that we are all savages at heart but observing a few amenities of civilized behavior." Then I went on to say: "I am afraid that I observe fewer of these amenities than you do. Reason? My back is to the wall and has been to the wall for so long that the pressure of my back on the wall has started to crumble the plaster that covers the bricks and mortar."

Isn't it odd that I said the wall was giving way, not my back? I think so. Pursuing this course of free association, I suddenly remembered a dinner date I once had with a distinguished colleague. During the course of this dinner, rather close to the end of it, he broke a long, mournful silence by lifting to me his sympathetic gaze and saying to me, sweetly, "Tennessee, don't you feel that you are blocked as a writer?"

I didn't stop to think of an answer; it came immediately off my tongue without any pause for planning. I said, "Oh, yes, I've always been blocked as a writer but my desire to write has been so strong that it has always broken down the block and gone past it."

Nothing untrue comes off the tongue that quickly. It is planned speeches that contain lies or dissimulations, not what you blurt out so spontaneously in one instant.

It was literally true. At the age of fourteen I discovered writing as an escape from a world of reality in which I felt acutely uncomfortable. It immediately became my place of retreat, my cave, my refuge. From what? From being called a sissy by the neighborhood kids, and Miss Nancy by my father, because I would rather read books in my grandfather's large and classical library than play marbles and baseball and other normal kid games, a result of a severe childhood illness and of excessive attachment to the female members of my family, who had coaxed me back into life.

I think no more than a week after I started writing I ran into the first block. It's hard to describe it in a way that will be understandable to anyone who is not a neurotic. I will try. All my life I have been haunted by the obsession that to desire a thing or to love a thing intensely is to place yourself in a vulnerable position, to be a possible, if not a probable, loser of what you most want. Let's leave it like that. That block has always been there and always will be, and my chance of getting, or achieving, anything that I long for will always be gravely reduced by the interminable existence of that block.

I described it once in a poem called "The Marvelous Children."

"He, the demon, set up barricades of gold and purple tinfoil, labeled Fear (and other august titles), which they, the children, would leap lightly over, always tossing backwards their wild laughter."

But having, always, to contend with this adversary of fear, which was sometimes terror, gave me a certain tendency toward an atmosphere of hysteria and violence in my writing, an atmosphere that has existed in it since the beginning.

In my first published work, for which I received the big sum of thirty-five dollars, a story published in the July or August issue of *Weird Tales* in the year 1928, I drew upon a paragraph in the ancient histories of Herodotus to create a story of how the Egyptian queen, Nitocris, invited all of her enemies to a lavish banquet in a subterranean hall on the shores of the Nile, and how, at the height of this banquet, she excused herself from the table and opened sluice gates admitting the waters of the Nile into the locked banquet hall, drowning her unloved guests like so many rats.

I was sixteen when I wrote this story, but already a confirmed writer, having entered upon this vocation at the age of fourteen, and, if you're well acquainted with my writings since then, I don't have to tell you that it set the keynote for most of the work that has followed.

My first four plays, two of them performed in St. Louis, were correspondingly violent or more so. My first play professionally produced and aimed at Broadway was *Battle of Angels* and it was about as violent as you can get on the stage.

During the nineteen years since then I have only produced five plays that are *not* violent: *The Glass Menagerie, You Touched Me, Summer and*

Smoke, The Rose Tattoo and, recently in Florida, a serious comedy called *Period of Adjustment,* which is still being worked on.

What surprises me is the degree to which both critics and audience have accepted this barrage of violence. I think I was surprised, most of all, by the acceptance and praise of *Suddenly Last Summer.* When it was done off Broadway, I thought I would be critically tarred and feathered and ridden on a fence rail out of the New York theatre, with no future haven except in translation for theatres abroad, who might mistakenly construe my work as a castigation of American morals, not understanding that I write about violence in American life only because I am not so well acquainted with the society of other countries.

Last year I thought it might help me as a writer to undertake psychoanalysis and so I did. The analyst, being acquainted with my work and recognizing the psychic wounds expressed in it, asked me, soon after we started, "Why are you so full of hate, anger and envy?"

Hate was the word I contested. After much discussion and argument, we decided that "hate" was just a provisional term and that we would only use it till we had discovered the more precise term. But unfortunately I got restless and started hopping back and forth between the analyst's couch and some Caribbean beaches. I think before we called it quits I had persuaded the doctor that hate was not the right word, that there was some other thing, some other word for it, which we had not yet uncovered, and we left it like that.

Anger, oh yes! And envy, yes! But not hate. I think that hate is a thing, a feeling, that can only exist where there is no understanding. Significantly, good physicians never have it. They never hate their patients, no matter how hateful their patients may seem to be, with their relentless, maniacal concentration on their own tortured egos.

Since I am a member of the human race, when I attack its behavior toward fellow members I am obviously including myself in the attack, unless I regard myself as not human but superior to humanity. I don't. In fact, I can't expose a human weakness on the stage unless I know it through having it myself. I have exposed a good many human weaknesses and brutalities and consequently I have them.

I don't even think that I am more conscious of mine than any of you are of yours. Guilt is universal. I mean a strong sense of guilt. If there exists any area in which a man can rise above his moral condition, imposed upon him at birth and long before birth, by the nature of his breed, then I think it is only a willingness to know it, to face its existence in him, and I think that at least below the conscious level, we all face it. Hence guilty feelings, and hence defiant aggressions, and hence the deep dark of despair that haunts our dreams, our creative work, and makes us distrust each other.

Enough of these philosophical abstractions, for now. To get back to writing for the theatre, if there is any truth in the Aristotelian idea that violence is purged by its poetic representation on a stage, then it may be that my cycle of violent plays have had a moral justification after all. I know that I have felt it. I have always felt a release from the sense of meaninglessness and death when a work of tragic intention has seemed to me to have achieved that intention, even if only approximately, nearly.

I would say that there is something much bigger in life and death than we have become aware of (or adequately recorded) in our living and dying. And, further, to compound this shameless romanticism, I would say that our serious theatre is a search for that something that is not yet successful but is still going on.

SWEET BIRD OF YOUTH

Relentless caper for all those who step
The legend of their youth into the noon.
—HART CRANE

TO CHERYL CRAWFORD

SYNOPSIS OF SCENES

ACT ONE

SCENE ONE:	A bedroom in the Royal Palms Hotel, somewhere on the Gulf Coast.
SCENE TWO:	The same. Later.

ACT TWO

SCENE ONE:	The terrace of Boss Finley's house in St. Cloud.
SCENE TWO:	The cocktail lounge and Palm Garden of the Royal Palms Hotel.

ACT THREE

The bedroom again.

TIME: Modern, an Easter Sunday, from late morning till late night.

SETTING and "SPECIAL EFFECTS" The stage is backed by a cyclorama that should give a poetic unity of mood to the several specific settings. There are nonrealistic projections on this "cyc," the most important and constant being a grove of royal palm trees. There is nearly always a wind among these very tall palm trees, sometimes loud, sometimes just a whisper, and sometimes it blends into a thematic music which will be identified, when it occurs, as "The Lament."

During the daytime scenes the cyclorama projection is a poetic abstraction of semitropical sea and sky in fair spring weather. At night it is the palm garden with its branches among the stars.

The specific settings should be treated as freely and sparingly as the sets for *Cat on a Hot Tin Roof* or *Summer and Smoke*. They'll be described as you come to them in the script.

Sweet Bird of Youth was presented at the Martin Beck Theatre in New York on March 10, 1959, by Cheryl Crawford. It was directed by Elia Kazan; the stage settings and lighting were by Jo Mielziner, the costumes by Anna Hill Johnstone, and the music by Paul Bowles; production stage manager, David Pardoll. The cast was as follows:

CHANCE WAYNE	Paul Newman
THE PRINCESS KOSMONOPOLIS	Geraldine Page
FLY	Milton J. Williams
MAID	Patricia Ripley
GEORGE SCUDDER	Logan Ramsey
HATCHER	John Napier
BOSS FINLEY	Sidney Blackmer
TOM JUNIOR	Rip Torn
AUNT NONNIE	Martine Bartlett
HEAVENLY FINLEY	Diana Hyland
CHARLES	Earl Sydnor
STUFF	Bruce Dern
MISS LUCY	Madeleine Sherwood
THE HECKLER	Charles Tyner
VIOLET	Monica May
EDNA	Hilda Brawner
SCOTTY	Charles McDaniel
BUD	Jim Jeter
MEN IN BAR	Duke Farley, Ron Harper, Kenneth Blake
PAGE	Glenn Stensel

ACT ONE

SCENE ONE

A bedroom of an old-fashioned but still fashionable hotel somewhere along the Gulf Coast in a town called St. Cloud. I think of it as resembling one of those "Grand Hotels" around Sorrento or Monte Carlo, set in a palm garden. The style is vaguely "Moorish." The principal set-piece is a great double bed which should be raked toward the audience. In a sort of Moorish corner backed by shuttered windows, is a wicker tabouret and two wicker stools, over which is suspended a Moorish lamp on a brass chain. The windows are floor length and they open out upon a gallery. There is also a practical door frame, opening onto a corridor: the walls are only suggested.

On the great bed are two figures, a sleeping woman, and a young man awake, sitting up, in the trousers of white silk pajamas. The sleeping woman's face is partly covered by an eyeless black satin domino to protect her from morning glare. She breathes and tosses on the bed as if in the grip of a nightmare. The young man is lighting his first cigarette of the day.

Outside the windows there is heard the soft, urgent cries of birds, the sound of their wings. Then a colored waiter, Fly, appears at door on the corridor, bearing coffee-service for two. He knocks. Chance rises, pauses a moment at a mirror in the fourth wall to run a comb through his slightly thinning blond hair before he crosses to open the door.

CHANCE: Aw, good, put it in there.

FLY: Yes, suh.

CHANCE: Give me the Bromo first. You better mix it for me, I'm—

FLY: Hands kind of shaky this mawnin'?

CHANCE [*shuddering after the Bromo*]: Open the shutters a little. Hey, I said a little, not much, not that much!

[*As the shutters are opened we see him clearly for the first time: he's in his late twenties and his face looks slightly older than that;*

you might describe it as a "ravaged young face" and yet it is still exceptionally good-looking. His body shows no decline, yet it's the kind of a body that white silk pajamas are, or ought to be, made for. A church bell tolls, and from another church, nearer, a choir starts singing the "Hallelujah Chorus." It draws him to the window, and as he crosses, he says:]

I didn't know it was—Sunday.

FLY: Yes, suh, it's *Easter* Sunday.

CHANCE [*leans out a moment, hands gripping the shutters*]: Uh-huh. . . .

FLY: That's the Episcopal Church they're singin' in. The bell's from the Catholic Church.

CHANCE: I'll put your tip on the check.

FLY: Thank you, Mr. Wayne.

CHANCE [*as Fly starts for the door*]: Hey. How did you know my name?

FLY: I waited tables in the Grand Ballroom when you used to come to the dances on Saturday nights, with that real pretty girl you used to dance so good with, Mr. Boss Finley's daughter?

CHANCE: I'm increasing your tip to five dollars in return for a favor, which is not to remember that you have recognized me or anything else at all. Your name is Fly—shoo, Fly. Close the door with no noise.

VOICE OUTSIDE: Just a minute.

CHANCE: Who's that?

VOICE OUTSIDE: George Scudder.

[*Slight pause. Fly exits.*]

CHANCE: How did you know I was here?

[*George Scudder enters: a coolly nice-looking, business-like young man who might be the head of the Junior Chamber of Commerce but is actually a young doctor, about thirty-six or -seven.*]

SCUDDER: The assistant manager that checked you in here last night phoned me this morning that you'd come back to St. Cloud.

CHANCE: So you came right over to welcome me home?

SCUDDER: Your lady friend sounds like she's coming out of ether.

CHANCE: The Princess had a rough night.

SCUDDER: You've latched onto a Princess? [*mockingly*] Gee.

CHANCE: She's traveling incognito.

SCUDDER: Golly, I should think she would, if she's checking in hotels with *you.*

CHANCE: George, you're the only man I know that still says "gee," "golly," and "gosh."

SCUDDER: Well, I'm not the sophisticated type, Chance.

CHANCE: That's for sure. Want some coffee?

SCUDDER: Nope. Just came for a talk. A quick one.

CHANCE: Okay. Start talking, man.

SCUDDER: Why've you come back to St. Cloud?

CHANCE: I've still got a mother and a girl in St. Cloud. How's Heavenly, George?

SCUDDER: We'll get around to that later. [*He glances at his watch.*] I've got to be in surgery at the hospital in twenty-five minutes.

CHANCE: You operate now, do you?

SCUDDER [*opening doctor's bag*]: I'm chief of staff there now.

CHANCE: Man, you've got it made.

SCUDDER: Why have you come back?

CHANCE: I heard that my mother was sick.

SCUDDER: But you said, "How's Heavenly," not "How's my mother," Chance. [*Chance sips coffee.*] Your mother died a couple of weeks ago. . . .

[*Chance slowly turns his back on the man and crosses to the window. Shadows of birds sweep the blind. He lowers it a little before he turns back to Scudder.*]

CHANCE: Why wasn't I notified?

SCUDDER: You were. A wire was sent you three days before she died at the last address she had for you, which was General Delivery, Los Angeles. We got no answer from that and another wire was sent you after she died, the same day of her death, and we got no response from that either. Here's the Church Record. The church took up a collection for her hospital and funeral expenses. She was buried nicely in your family plot and the church has also given her a very nice headstone. I'm giving you these details in spite of the fact that I know and everyone here in town knows that you had no interest in her, less than people who knew her only slightly, such as myself.

CHANCE: How did she go?

SCUDDER: She had a long illness, Chance. You know about that.

CHANCE: Yes. She was sick when I left here the last time.

SCUDDER: She was sick at heart as well as sick in her body at that time, Chance. But people were very good to her, especially people who knew her in church, and the Reverend Walker was with her at the end.

[*Chance sits down on the bed. He puts out his unfinished cigarette and immediately lights another. His voice becomes thin and strained.*]

CHANCE: She never had any luck.

SCUDDER: Luck? Well, that's all over with now. If you want to know anything more about that, you can get in touch with Reverend Walker about it, although I'm afraid he won't be likely to show much cordiality to you.

CHANCE: She's gone. Why talk about it?

SCUDDER: I hope you haven't forgotten the letter I wrote you soon after you last left town.

CHANCE: No. I got no letter.

SCUDDER: I wrote you in care of an address your mother gave me about a very important private matter.

CHANCE: I've been moving a lot.

SCUDDER: I didn't even mention names in the letter.

CHANCE: What was the letter about?

SCUDDER: Sit over here so I don't have to talk loud about this. Come over here. I can't talk loud about this. [*Scudder indicates the chair by the tabouret. Chance crosses and rests a foot on the chair.*] In this letter I just told you that a certain girl we know had to go through an awful experience, a tragic ordeal, because of past contact with you. I told you that I was only giving you this information so that you would know better than to come back to St. Cloud, but you didn't know better.

CHANCE: I told you I got no letter. Don't tell me about a letter, I didn't get any letter.

SCUDDER: I'm telling you what I told you in this letter.

CHANCE: All right. Tell me what you told me, don't—don't talk to me like a club, a chamber of something. What did you tell me? What ordeal? What girl? Heavenly? Heavenly? George?

SCUDDER: I see it's not going to be possible to talk about this quietly and so I . . .

CHANCE [*rising to block Scudder's way*]: Heavenly? What ordeal?

SCUDDER: We will not mention names. Chance, I rushed over here this morning as soon as I heard you were back in St. Cloud, before the girl's father and brother could hear that you were back in St. Cloud, to stop you from trying to get in touch with the girl and to get out of here. That is absolutely all I have to say to you in this room at this moment. . . . But I hope I have said it in a way to impress you with the vital urgency of it, so you will leave. . . .

CHANCE: Jesus! If something's happened to Heavenly, will you please tell me—what?

SCUDDER: I said no names. We are not alone in this room. Now when I go downstairs now, I'll speak to Dan Hatcher, assistant manager here . . . he told me you'd checked in here . . . and tell him you want to check out, so you'd better get Sleeping Beauty and yourself ready to travel, and I suggest that you keep on traveling till you've crossed the state line. . . .

CHANCE: You're not going to leave this room till you've explained to me what you've been hinting at about my girl in St. Cloud.

SCUDDER: There's a lot more to this which we feel ought not to be talked about to anyone, least of all to you, since you have turned into a criminal degenerate, the only right term for you, but, Chance, I think I ought to remind you that once long ago, the father of this girl wrote out a prescription for you, a sort of medical prescription, which is castration. You'd better think about that, that would deprive you of all you've got to get by on. [*He moves toward the steps.*]

CHANCE: I'm used to that threat. I'm not going to leave St. Cloud without my girl.

SCUDDER [*on the steps*]: You don't have a girl in St. Cloud. Heavenly and I are going to be married next month. [*He leaves abruptly.*]

[*Chance, shaken by what he has heard, turns and picks up phone, and kneels on the floor.*]

CHANCE: Hello? St. Cloud 525. Hello, Aunt Nonnie? This is Chance, yes Chance. I'm staying at the Royal Palms and I . . . what's the matter, has something happened to Heavenly? Why can't you talk now? George Scudder was here and . . . Aunt Nonnie? Aunt Nonnie?

[*The other end hangs up. The sleeping woman suddenly cries out in her sleep. Chance drops the phone on its cradle and runs to the bed.*]

CHANCE [*bending over her as she struggles out of a nightmare*]: Princess! Princess! Hey, *Princess Kos!* [*He removes her eyemask; she sits up gasping and staring wild-eyed about her.*]

PRINCESS: Who are you? Help!

CHANCE [*on the bed*]: Hush now. . . .

PRINCESS: Oh . . . I . . . had . . . a *terrible* dream.

CHANCE: It's all right. Chance's with you.

PRINCESS: Who?

CHANCE: Me.

PRINCESS: I don't know who you are!

CHANCE: You'll remember soon, Princess.

PRINCESS: I don't know, I don't know. . . .

CHANCE: It'll come back to you soon. What are you reachin' for, honey?

PRINCESS: Oxygen! Mask!

CHANCE: Why? Do you feel short-winded?

PRINCESS Yes! I have . . . air . . . shortage!

CHANCE [*looking for the correct piece of luggage*]: Which bag is your oxygen in? I can't remember which bag we packed it in. Aw, yeah, the crocodile case, the one with the combination lock. Wasn't the first number zero . . . [*He comes back to the bed, and reaches for a bag under its far side.*]

PRINCESS [*as if with her dying breath*]: Zero, zero. Two zeros to the right and then back around to . . .

CHANCE: Zero, three zeros, two of them to the right and the last one to the left. . . .

PRINCESS: Hurry! I can't breathe, I'm dying!

CHANCE: I'm getting it, Princess.

PRINCESS: HURRY!

CHANCE: Here we are, I've got it. . . .

[*He has extracted from case a small oxygen cylinder and mask. He fits the inhalator over her nose and mouth. She falls back on the pillow. He places the other pillow under her head. After a moment, her panicky breath subsiding, she growls at him.*]

PRINCESS: Why in hell did you lock it up in that case?

CHANCE [*standing at the head of the bed*]: You said to put all your valuables in that case.

PRINCESS: I meant my jewelry, and you know it, you, bastard!

CHANCE: Princess, I didn't think you'd have these attacks any more. I thought that having me with you to protect you would stop these attacks of panic, I . . .

PRINCESS: Give me a pill.

CHANCE: Which pill?

PRINCESS: A pink one, a pinkie, and vodka . . .

[*He puts the tank on the floor, and goes over to the trunk. The phone rings. Chance gives the Princess a pill, picks up the vodka bottle and goes to the phone. He sits down with the bottle between his knees.*]

CHANCE [*pouring a drink, phone held between shoulder and ear*]: Hello? Oh, hello, Mr. Hatcher——Oh? But Mr. Hatcher, when we checked in here last night we weren't told that, and Miss Alexandra Del Lago . . .

PRINCESS [*shouting*]: *Don't use my name!*

CHANCE: . . . is suffering from exhaustion, she's not at all well, Mr. Hatcher, and certainly not in any condition to travel. . . . I'm sure you don't want to take the responsibility for what might happen to Miss Del Lago . . .

PRINCESS [*shouting again*]: *Don't use my name!*

CHANCE: . . . if she attempted to leave here today in the condition she's in . . . do you?

PRINCESS: *Hang up!* [*He does. He comes over with his drink and the bottle to the Princess.*] I want to forget everything, I want to forget who I am. . . .

CHANCE [*handing her the drink*]: He said that . . .

PRINCESS [*drinking*]: Please shut up, I'm *forgetting!*

CHANCE [*taking the glass from her*]: Okay, go on forget. There's nothing better than that, I wish I could do it. . . .

PRINCESS: I can, I will. I'm forgetting . . . I'm forgetting. . . .

[*She lies down. Chance moves to the foot of the bed, where he seems to be struck with an idea. He puts the bottle down on the floor, runs to the chaise and picks up a tape recorder. Taking it back to the bed, he places the recorder on the floor. As he plugs it in, he coughs.*]

What's going on?

CHANCE: Looking for my toothbrush.

PRINCESS [*throwing the oxygen mask on the bed*]: Will you please take that away.

CHANCE: Sure you've had enough of it?

PRINCESS [*laughs breathlessly*]: Yes, for God's sake, take it away. I must look hideous in it.

CHANCE [*taking the mask*]: No, no, you just look exotic, like a princess from Mars or a big magnified insect.

PRINCESS: Thank you, check the cylinder please.

CHANCE: For what?

PRINCESS: Check the air left in it; there's a gauge on the cylinder that gives the pressure. . . .

CHANCE: You're still breathing like a quarter horse that's been run a full mile. Are you sure you don't want a doctor?

PRINCESS: No, for God's sake . . . no!

CHANCE: Why are you so scared of doctors?

PRINCESS [*hoarsely, quickly*]: I don't need them. What happened is nothing at all. It happens frequently to me. Something disturbs me . . . adrenalin's pumped in my blood and I get short-winded, that's all, that's all there is to it . . . I woke up, I didn't know where I was or who I was with, I got panicky . . . adrenalin was released and I got short-winded. . . .

CHANCE: Are you okay now, Princess? Huh? [*He kneels on the bed, and helps straighten up the pillows.*]

PRINCESS: Not quite yet, but I will be. I will be.

CHANCE: You're full of complexes, plump lady.

PRINCESS: What did you call me?

CHANCE: Plump lady.

PRINCESS: Why do you call me that? Have I let go of my figure?

CHANCE: You put on a good deal of weight after that disappointment you had last month.

PRINCESS [*hitting him with a small pillow*]: What disappointment? I don't remember any.

CHANCE: Can you control your memory like that?

PRINCESS: Yes. I've had to learn to. What is this place, a hospital? And you, what are you, a male nurse?

CHANCE: I take care of you but I'm not your nurse.

PRINCESS: But you're employed by me, aren't you? For some purpose or other?

CHANCE: I'm not on salary with you.

PRINCESS: What are you on? Just expenses?

CHANCE: Yep. You're footing the bills.

PRINCESS: I see. Yes, I see.

CHANCE: Why're you rubbing your eyes?

PRINCESS: My vision's so cloudy! Don't I wear glasses, don't I have any glasses?

CHANCE: You had a little accident with your glasses.

PRINCESS: What was that?

CHANCE: You fell on your face with them on.

PRINCESS: Were they completely demolished?

CHANCE: One lens cracked.

PRINCESS: Well, please give me the remnants. I don't mind waking up in an intimate situation with someone, but I like to see who it's with, so I can make whatever adjustment seems called for. . . .

CHANCE [*rises and goes to the trunk, where he lights cigarette*]: You know what I look like.

PRINCESS: No, I don't.

CHANCE: You did.

PRINCESS: I tell you I don't remember, it's all gone away!

CHANCE: I don't believe in amnesia.

PRINCESS: Neither do I. But you have to believe a thing that happens to you.

CHANCE: Where did I put your glasses?

PRINCESS: Don't ask me. You say I fell on them. If I was in that condition I wouldn't be likely to know where anything is I had with me. What happened last night?

[*He has picked them up but not given them to her.*]

CHANCE: You knocked yourself out.

PRINCESS: Did we sleep here together?

CHANCE: Yes, but I didn't molest you.

PRINCESS: Should I thank you for that, or accuse you of cheating? [*She laughs sadly.*]

CHANCE: I like you, you're a nice monster.

PRINCESS: Your voice sounds young. Are you young?

CHANCE: My age is twenty-nine years.

PRINCESS: That's young for anyone but an Arab. Are you very good-looking?

CHANCE: I used to be the best-looking boy in this town.

PRINCESS: How large is the town?

CHANCE: Fair-sized.

PRINCESS: Well, I like a good mystery novel, I read them to put me to sleep and if they don't put me to sleep, they're good; but this one's a little too good for comfort. I wish you would find me my glasses. . . .

[*He reaches over headboard to hand the glasses to her. She puts them on and looks him over. Then she motions him to come nearer and touches his bare chest with her finger tips.*]

Well, I may have done better, but God knows I've done worse.

CHANCE: What are you doing now, Princess?

PRINCESS: The tactile approach.

CHANCE: You do that like you were feeling a piece of goods to see if it was genuine silk or phony. . . .

PRINCESS: It feels like silk. Genuine! This much I do remember, that I like bodies to be hairless, silky-smooth gold!

CHANCE: Do I meet these requirements?

PRINCESS: You seem to meet those requirements. But I still have a feeling that something is not satisfied in the relation between us.

CHANCE [*moving away from her*]: You've had your experiences, I've had mine. You can't expect everything to be settled at once. . . . Two different experiences of two different people. Naturally there's some things that have to be settled between them before there's any absolute agreement.

PRINCESS [*throwing the glasses on the bed*]: Take that splintered lens out before it gets in my eye.

CHANCE [*obeying this instruction by knocking the glasses sharply on the bed table*]: You like to give orders, don't you?

PRINCESS: It's something I seem to be used to.

CHANCE: How would you like to *take* them? To be a slave?

PRINCESS: What time is it?

CHANCE: My watch is in hock somewhere. Why don't you look at yours?

PRINCESS: Where's mine?

[*He reaches lazily over to the table, and hands it to her.*]

CHANCE: It's stopped, at five past seven.

PRINCESS: Surely it's later than that, or earlier, that's no hour when I'm . . .

CHANCE: Platinum, is it?

PRINCESS: No, it's only white gold. I never travel with anything very expensive.

CHANCE: Why? Do you get robbed much? Huh? Do you get "rolled" often?

PRINCESS: Get what?

CHANCE: "Rolled." Isn't that expression in your vocabulary?

PRINCESS: Give me the phone.

CHANCE: For what?

PRINCESS: I said give me the phone.

CHANCE: I know. And I said for what?

PRINCESS: I want to enquire where I am and who is with me?

CHANCE: Take it easy.

PRINCESS: Will you give me the phone?

CHANCE: Relax. You're getting short-winded again. . . . [*He takes hold of her shoulders.*]

PRINCESS: Please let go of me.

CHANCE: Don't you feel secure with me? Lean back. Lean back against me.

PRINCESS: Lean back?

CHANCE: This way, this way. There . . .

[*He pulls her into his arms: She rests in them, panting a little like a trapped rabbit.*]

PRINCESS: It gives you an awful trapped feeling this, this memory block. . . . I feel as if someone I loved had died lately, and I don't want to remember who it could be.

CHANCE: Do you remember your name?

PRINCESS: Yes, I do.

CHANCE: What's your name?

PRINCESS: I think there's some reason why I prefer not to tell you.

CHANCE: Well, I happen to know it. You registered under a phony name in Palm Beach but I discovered your real one. And you admitted it to me.

PRINCESS: I'm the Princess Kosmonopolis.

CHANCE: Yes, and you used to be known as . . .

PRINCESS [*sits up sharply*]: No, stop . . . will you let me do it? Quietly, in my own way? The last place I remember . . .

CHANCE: What's the last place you remember?

PRINCESS: A town with the crazy name of Tallahassee.

CHANCE: Yeah. We drove through there. That's where I reminded you that today would be Sunday and we ought to lay in a supply of liquor to get us through it without us being dehydrated too severely, and so we stopped there but it was a college town and we had some trouble locating a package store, open. . . .

PRINCESS: But we did, did we?

CHANCE [*getting up for the bottle and pouring her a drink*]: Oh, sure, we bought three bottles of vodka. You curled up in the back seat with one of those bottles and when I looked back you were blotto. I intended to stay on the Old Spanish Trail straight through to Texas, where you had some oil wells to look at. I didn't stop here . . . I was stopped.

PRINCESS: What by, a cop? Or . . .

CHANCE: No. No cop, but I was arrested by something.

PRINCESS: My car. Where is my car?

CHANCE [*handing her the drink*]: In the hotel parking lot, Princess.

PRINCESS: Oh, then, this is a hotel?

CHANCE: It's the elegant old Royal Palms Hotel in the town of St. Cloud.

[*Gulls fly past window, shadows sweeping the blind: they cry out with soft urgency.*]

PRINCESS: Those pigeons out there sound hoarse. They sound like gulls to me. Of course, they could be pigeons with laryngitis.

[*Chance glances at her with his flickering smile and laughs softly.*]

Will you help me please? I'm about to get up.

CHANCE: What do you want? I'll get it.

PRINCESS: I want to go to the window.

CHANCE: What for?

PRINCESS: To look out of it.

CHANCE: I can describe the view to you.

PRINCESS: I'm not sure I'd trust your description. WELL?

CHANCE: Okay, *oopsa-daisy.*

PRINCESS: My God! I said help me up, not . . . toss me onto the carpet! [*Sways dizzily a moment, clutching bed. Then draws a breath and crosses to the window.*]

[*Pauses as she gazes out, squinting into noon's brilliance.*]

CHANCE: Well, what do you see? Give me your description of the view, Princess?

PRINCESS [*faces the audience*]: I see a palm garden.

CHANCE: And a four-lane highway just past it.

PRINCESS [*squinting and shielding her eyes*]: Yes, I see that and a strip of beach with some bathers and then, an infinite stretch of nothing but water and . . . [*She cries out softly and turns away from the window.*]

CHANCE: What? . . .

PRINCESS: Oh God, I remember the thing I wanted not to. The goddam end of my life! [*She draws a deep shuddering breath.*]

CHANCE [*running to her aid*]: What's the matter?

PRINCESS: Help me back to bed. Oh God, no wonder I didn't want to remember, I was no fool!

[*He assists her to the bed. There is an unmistakable sympathy in his manner, however shallow.*]

CHANCE: Oxygen?

PRINCESS [*draws another deep shuddering breath*]: No! Where's the stuff? Did you leave it in the car?

CHANCE: Oh, the stuff? Under the mattress. [*Moving to the other side of the bed, he pulls out a small pouch.*]

PRINCESS: A stupid place to put it.

CHANCE [*sits at the foot of the bed*]: What's wrong with under the mattress?

PRINCESS [*sits up on the edge of the bed*]: There's such a thing as chambermaids in the world, they make up beds, they come across lumps in a mattress.

CHANCE: This isn't pot. What is it?

PRINCESS: Wouldn't that be pretty? A year in jail in one of those model prisons for distinguished addicts. What is it? Don't you know what it is, you beautiful, stupid young man? It's hashish, Moroccan, the finest.

CHANCE: Oh, hash! How'd you get it through customs when you came back for your comeback?

PRINCESS: I didn't get it through customs. The ship's doctor gave me injections while this stuff was winging over the ocean to a shifty young gentleman who thought he could blackmail me for it. [*She puts on her slippers with a vigorous gesture.*]

CHANCE: Couldn't he?

PRINCESS: Of course not. I called his bluff.

CHANCE: You took injections coming over?

PRINCESS: With my neuritis? I had to. Come on give it to me.

CHANCE: Don't you want it packed right?

PRINCESS: You talk too much. You ask too many questions. I need something quick. [*She rises.*]

CHANCE: I'm a new hand at this.

PRINCESS: I'm sure, or you wouldn't discuss it in a hotel room. . . .

[*She turns to the audience, and intermittently changes the focus of her attention.*]

For years they all told me that it was ridiculous of me to feel that I couldn't go back to the screen or the stage as a middle-aged woman. They told me I was an artist, not just a star whose career depended on youth. But I knew in my heart that the legend of Alexandra del Lago couldn't be separated from an appearance of youth. . . .

There's no more valuable knowledge than knowing the right time to go. I knew it. I went at the right time to go. RETIRED! Where to? To what? To that dead planet the moon. . . .

There's nowhere else to retire to when you retire from an art because, believe it or not, I really was once an artist. So I retired to the moon, but the atmosphere of the moon doesn't have any oxygen in it. I began to feel breathless, in that withered, withering country, of time coming after time not meant to come after, and so I discovered . . . Haven't you fixed it yet?

[*Chance rises and goes to her with a cigarette he has been preparing.*]

Discovered this!

And other practices like it, to put to sleep the tiger that raged in my nerves. . . . Why the unsatisfied tiger? In the nerves jungle? Why is anything, anywhere, unsatisfied, and raging? . . .

Ask somebody's good doctor. But don't believe his answer because it isn't . . . the answer . . . if I had just been old but you see, I wasn't old. . . .

I just wasn't young, not young, young. I just wasn't young anymore. . . .

CHANCE: Nobody's young anymore. . . .

PRINCESS: But you see, I couldn't get old with that tiger still in me raging.

CHANCE: Nobody can get old. . . .

PRINCESS: Stars in retirement sometimes give acting lessons. Or take up painting, paint flowers on pots, or landscapes. I could have painted the landscape of the endless, withering country in which I wandered like a lost nomad. If I could paint deserts and nomads, if I could paint . . . hahaha. . . .

CHANCE: SH-Sh-sh-

PRINCESS: Sorry!

CHANCE: Smoke.

PRINCESS: Yes, smoke! And then the young lovers. . . .

CHANCE: Me?

PRINCESS: You? Yes, finally you. But you come after the comeback. Ha . . . Ha . . . The glorious comeback, when I turned fool and came back. . . . The screen's a very clear mirror. There's a thing called a close-up. The camera advances and you stand still and your head, your face, is caught in the frame of the picture with a light blazing on it and all your terrible history screams while you smile. . . .

CHANCE: How do you know? Maybe it wasn't a failure, maybe you were just scared, just chicken, Princess . . . ha-ha-ha. . . .

PRINCESS: Not a failure . . . after that close-up they gasped. . . . People gasped. . . . I heard them whisper, their shocked whispers. Is that her? Is that her? Her? . . . I made the mistake of wearing a very elaborate gown to the *première,* a gown with a train that had to be gathered up as I rose from my seat and began the interminable retreat from the city of flames, up, up, up the unbearably long theatre aisle, gasping for breath and still clutching up the regal white train of my gown, all the way up the forever . . . length of the aisle, and behind me some small unknown man grabbing at me, saying, stay, stay! At last the top of the aisle, I turned and struck him, then let the train fall, forgot it, and tried to run down the marble stairs, tripped of course, fell and, rolled, rolled, like a sailor's drunk whore to the bottom . . . hands, merciful hands without faces, assisted me to get up. After that? Flight, just flight, not interrupted until I woke up this morning. . . . Oh God it's gone out. . . .

CHANCE: Let me fix you another. Huh? Shall I fix you another?

PRINCESS: Let me finish yours. You can't retire with the out-crying heart of an artist still crying out, in your body, in your nerves, in your what? Heart? Oh, no that's gone, that's . . .

CHANCE [*He goes to her, takes the cigarette out of her hand and gives her a fresh one.*] Here, I've fixed you another one . . . Princess, I've fixed you another. . . . [*He sits on the floor, leaning against the foot of the bed.*]

PRINCESS: Well, sooner or later, at some point in your life, the thing that you lived for is lost or abandoned, and then . . . you die, or find something else. This is my something else. . . . [*She approaches the bed.*] And ordinarily I take the most fantastic precautions against . . . detection. . . . [*She sits on the bed, then lies down on her back, her head over the foot, near his.*] I cannot imagine what possessed me to let you know. Knowing so little about you as I seem to know.

CHANCE: I must've inspired a good deal of confidence in you.

PRINCESS: If that's the case, I've gone crazy. Now tell me something. What is that body of water, that sea, out past the palm garden and four-lane highway? I ask you because I remember now that we turned west from the sea when we went onto that highway called the Old Spanish Trail.

CHANCE: We've come back to the sea.

PRINCESS: What sea?

CHANCE: The Gulf.

PRINCESS: The Gulf?

CHANCE: The Gulf of misunderstanding between me and you. . . .

PRINCESS: We don't understand each other? And lie here smoking this stuff?

CHANCE: Princess, don't forget that this stuff is yours, that you provided me with it.

PRINCESS: What are you trying to prove? [*Church bells toll.*] Sundays go on a long time.

CHANCE: You don't deny it was yours.

PRINCESS: What's mine?

CHANCE: You brought it into the country, you smuggled it through customs into the U.S.A. and you had a fair supply of it at that hotel in Palm Beach and were asked to check out before you were ready to do so, because its aroma drifted into the corridor one breezy night.

PRINCESS: What are you trying to prove?

CHANCE: You don't deny that you introduced me to it?

PRINCESS: Boy, I doubt very much that I have any vice that I'd need to introduce to you. . . .

CHANCE: Don't call me "boy."

PRINCESS: Why not?

CHANCE: It sounds condescending. And all my vices were caught from other people.

PRINCESS: What are you trying to prove? My memory's come back now. Excessively clearly. It was this mutual practice that brought us together. When you came in my cabana to give me one of those papaya cream rubs, you sniffed, you grinned and said you'd like a stick too.

CHANCE: That's right. I knew the smell of it.

PRINCESS: What are you trying to prove?

CHANCE: You asked me four or five times what I'm trying to prove, the answer is nothing. I'm just making sure that your memory's cleared up now. You do remember me coming in your cabana to give you those papaya cream rubs?

PRINCESS: Of course I do, Carl!

CHANCE: My name is not Carl. It's Chance.

PRINCESS: You called yourself Carl.

CHANCE: I always carry an extra name in my pocket.

PRINCESS: You're not a criminal, are you?

CHANCE: No ma'am, not me. You're the one that's committed a federal offense.

[*She stares at him a moment, and then goes to the door leading to the hall, looks out and listens.*]

What did you do that for?

PRINCESS [*closing the door*]: To see if someone was planted outside the door.

CHANCE: You still don't trust me?

PRINCESS: Someone that gives me a false name?

CHANCE: You registered under a phony one in Palm Beach.

PRINCESS: Yes, to avoid getting any reports or condolences on the disaster I ran from. [*She crosses to the window. There is a pause followed by "The Lament."*] And so we've not arrived at any agreement?

CHANCE: No ma'am, not a complete one.

[*She turns her back to the window and gazes at him from there.*]

PRINCESS: What's the gimmick? The hitch?

CHANCE: The usual one.

PRINCESS: What's that?

CHANCE: Doesn't somebody always hold out for something?

PRINCESS: Are you holding out for something?

CHANCE: Uh-huh. . . .

PRINCESS: What?

CHANCE: You said that you had a large block of stock, more than half ownership in a sort of a second-rate Hollywood studio, and could put me under contract. I doubted your word about that. You're not like any phony I've met before, but phonies come in all types and sizes. So I held out, even after we locked your cabana door for the papaya cream rubs. . . . You wired for some contract papers we signed. It was notarized and witnessed by three strangers found in a bar.

PRINCESS: Then why did you hold out, still?

CHANCE: I didn't have much faith in it. You know, you can buy those things for six bits in novelty stores. I've been conned and tricked too often to put much faith in anything that could still be phony.

PRINCESS: You're wise. However, I have the impression that there's been a certain amount of intimacy between us.

CHANCE: A certain amount. No more. I wanted to hold your interest.

PRINCESS: Well, you miscalculated. My interest always increases with satisfaction.

CHANCE: Then you're unusual in that respect, too.

PRINCESS: In all respects I'm not common.

CHANCE: But I guess the contract we signed is full of loopholes?

PRINCESS: Truthfully, yes, it is. I can get out of it if I wanted to. And so can the studio. Do you have any talent?

CHANCE: For what?

PRINCESS: Acting, baby, ACTING!

CHANCE: I'm not as positive of it as I once was. I've had more chances than I could count on my fingers, and made the grade almost, but not quite, every time. Something always blocks me. . . .

PRINCESS: What? What? Do you *know*? [*He rises. "The Lamentation" is heard very faintly.*] *Fear?*

CHANCE: No not fear, but terror . . . otherwise would I be your goddam caretaker, hauling you across the country? Picking you up when you fall? Well would I? Except for that block, by anything less than a star?

PRINCESS: CARL!

CHANCE: Chance. . . . Chance Wayne. You're stoned.

PRINCESS: Chance, come back to your youth. Put off this false, ugly hardness and . . .

CHANCE: And be took in by every con-merchant I meet?

PRINCESS: I'm not a phony, believe me.

CHANCE: Well, then, what is it you want? Come on say it, Princess.

PRINCESS: Chance, come here. [*He smiles but doesn't move.*] Come here and let's comfort each other a little. [*He crouches by the bed; she encircles him with her bare arms.*]

CHANCE: Princess! Do you know something? All this conversation has been recorded on tape?

PRINCESS: What are you talking about?

CHANCE: Listen. I'll play it back to you. [*He uncovers the tape recorder; approaches her with the earpiece.*]

PRINCESS: How did you get that thing?

CHANCE: You bought it for me in Palm Beach. I said that I wanted it to improve my diction. . . .

[*He presses the "play" button on the recorder. The following in the left column can either be on a public address system, or can be cut.*]

(PLAYBACK)

PRINCESS: What is it? Don't you know what it is? You stupid, beautiful young man. It's hashish, Moroccan, the finest.

CHANCE: Oh, hash? How'd you get it through customs when you came back for your "comeback"?

PRINCESS: I didn't get it through customs. The ship's doctor. . . .

(LIVE)

PRINCESS: What a smart cookie you are.

CHANCE: How does it feel to be over a great big barrel?

[*He snaps off the recorder and picks up the reels.*]

PRINCESS: This is blackmail is it? Where's my mink stole?

CHANCE: Not stolen.

[*He tosses it to her contemptuously from a chair.*]

PRINCESS: Where is my jewel case?

CHANCE [*picks it up off the floor and throws it on the bed*]: Here.

PRINCESS [*opens it up and starts to put on some jewelry*]: Every piece is insured and described in detail. Lloyd's in London.

CHANCE: *Who's* a smart cookie, Princess? You want your purse now so you can count your money?

PRINCESS: I don't carry currency with me, just travelers' checks.

CHANCE: I noted that fact already. But I got a fountain pen you can sign them with.

PRINCESS: Ho, ho!

CHANCE: "Ho, ho!" What an insincere laugh, if that's how you fake a laugh, no wonder you didn't make good in your comeback picture. . . .

PRINCESS: Are you serious about this attempt to blackmail me?

CHANCE: You'd better believe it. Your trade's turned dirt on you, Princess. You understand that language?

PRINCESS: The language of the gutter is understood anywhere that anyone ever fell in it.

CHANCE: Aw, then you *do* understand.

PRINCESS: And if I shouldn't comply with this order of yours?

CHANCE: You still got a name, you're still a personage, Princess. You wouldn't want "Confidential" or "Whisper" or "Hush-Hush" or the narcotics department of the F.B.I. to get hold of one of these tape-records, would you? And I'm going to make lots of copies. Huh? Princess?

PRINCESS: You are trembling and sweating . . . you see this part doesn't suit you, you just don't play it well, Chance. . . . [*Chance puts the reels in a suitcase.*] I hate to think of what kind of desperation has made you try to intimidate me, ME? ALEXANDRA DEL LAGO? with that ridiculous threat. Why it's so silly, it's touching, downright endearing, it makes me feel close to you, Chance.

You were well born, weren't you? Born of good Southern stock, in a genteel tradition, with just one disadvantage, a laurel wreath on your forehead, given too early, without enough effort to earn it . . . where's your scrapbook, Chance? [*He crosses to the bed, takes a travelers' checkbook out of her purse, and extends it to her.*] Where's your book full of little theatre notices and stills that show you in the background of . . .

CHANCE: Here! Here! Start signing . . . or . . .

PRINCESS [*pointing to the bathroom*]: Or WHAT? Go take a shower under cold water. I don't like hot sweaty bodies in a tropical climate. Oh, you, I do want and will accept, still . . . under certain conditions which I will make very clear to you.

CHANCE: Here. [*Throws the checkbook toward the bed.*]

PRINCESS: Put this away. And your leaky fountain pen . . . When monster meets monster, one monster has to give way, AND IT WILL NEVER BE ME. I'm an older hand at it . . . with much more natural aptitude at it than you have. . . . Now then, you put the cart a little in front of the horse. Signed checks are payment, delivery comes first. Certainly I can afford it, I could deduct you, as my caretaker, Chance, remember that I was a star before big taxes . . . and had a husband who was a great merchant prince. He taught me to deal with money. . . . Now, Chance, please pay close attention while I tell you the very special conditions under which I will keep you in my employment . . . after this miscalculation. . . .

Forget the legend that I was and the ruin of that legend.

Whether or not I do have a disease of the heart that places an early terminal date on my life, no mention of that, no reference to it ever. No mention of death, never, never a word on that odious subject. I've been accused of having a death wish but I think it's life that I wish for, terribly, shamelessly, on any terms whatsoever.

When I say now, the answer must not be later. I have only one way to forget these things I don't want to remember and that's through the act of love-making. That's the only dependable distraction so when I say now, because I need that distraction, it has to be now, not later.

[*She crosses to the bed: He rises from the opposite side of the bed and goes to the window: She gazes at his back as he looks out the window. Pause: "The Lamentation."*]

[*Princess, finally, softly.*]

Chance, I need that distraction. It's time for me to find out if you're able to give it to me. You mustn't hang onto your silly little idea that you can increase your value by turning away and looking out a window when somebody wants you. . . . I want you. . . . I say now and I mean now, then and not until then will I call downstairs and tell the hotel cashier that I'm sending a young man down with some travelers' checks to cash for me. . . .

CHANCE [*turning slowly from the window*]: Aren't you ashamed, a little?

PRINCESS: Of course I am. Aren't you?

CHANCE: More than a little. . . .

PRINCESS: Close the shutters, draw the curtain across them.

[*He obeys these commands.*]

Now get a little sweet music on the radio and come here to me and make me almost believe that we're a pair of young lovers without any shame.

SCENE TWO

As the curtain rises, the Princess has a fountain pen in hand and is signing checks. Chance, now wearing dark slacks, socks and shoes of the fashionable loafer type, is putting on his shirt and speaks as the curtain opens.

CHANCE: Keep on writing, has the pen gone dry?

PRINCESS: I started at the back of the book where the big ones are.

CHANCE: Yes, but you stopped too soon.

PRINCESS: All right, one more from the front of the book as a token of some satisfaction. I said some, not complete.

CHANCE [*picking up the phone*]: Operator—give me the cashier please.

PRINCESS: What are you doing that for?

CHANCE: You have to tell the cashier you're sending me down with some travelers' checks to cash for you.

PRINCESS: Have to? Did you say have to?

CHANCE: Cashier? Just a moment. The Princess Kosmonopolis. [*He thrusts the phone at her.*]

PRINCESS [*into the phone*]: Who is this? But I don't want the cashier. My watch has stopped and I want to know the right time . . . five after three? Thank you . . . he says it's five after three. [*She hangs up and smiles at Chance.*] I'm not ready to be left alone in this room. Now let's not fight any more over little points like that, let's save our strength for the big ones. I'll have the checks cashed for you as soon as I've put on my face. I just don't want to be left alone in this place till I've put on the face that I face the world with, baby. Maybe after we get to know each other, we won't fight over little points any more, the struggle will stop, maybe we won't even fight over big points, baby. Will you open the shutters a little bit please? [*He doesn't seem to hear her. "The Lament" is heard.*] I won't be able to see my face in the mirror. . . . Open the shutters, I won't be able to see my face in the mirror.

CHANCE: Do you want to?

PRINCESS [*pointing*]: Unfortunately I have to! Open the shutters!

[*He does. He remains by the open shutters, looking out as "The Lament" in the air continues.*]

CHANCE: —I was born in this town. I was born in St. Cloud.

PRINCESS: That's a good way to begin to tell your life story. Tell me your life story. I'm interested in it, I really would like to know it. Let's make it your audition, a sort of screen test for you. I can watch you in the mirror while I put my face on. And tell me your life story, and if you hold my attention with your life story, I'll know you have talent, I'll wire my studio on the Coast that I'm still alive and I'm on my way to the Coast with a young man named Chance Wayne that I think is cut out to be a great young star.

CHANCE [*moving out on the forestage*]: Here is the town I was born in, and lived in till ten years ago, in St. Cloud. I was a twelve-pound baby, normal and healthy, but with some kind of quantity "X" in my blood, a wish or a need to be different. . . . The kids that I grew up with are mostly still here and what they call "settled down," gone into business, married and bringing up children, the little crowd I was in with, that I used to be the star of, was the snob set, the ones with the big names and money. I didn't have either . . . [*The Princess utters a soft laugh in her dimmed-out area.*] What I had was . . . [*The Princess half turns, brush poised in a faint, dusty beam of light.*]

PRINCESS: BEAUTY! Say it! Say it! What you had was beauty! I had it! I say it, with pride, no matter how sad, being gone, now.

CHANCE: Yes, well . . . the others . . . [*The Princess resumes brushing hair and the sudden cold beam of light on her goes out again.*] . . . are all now members of the young social set here. The girls are young matrons, bridge-players, and the boys belong to the Junior Chamber of Commerce and some of them, clubs in New Orleans such as Rex and Comus and ride on the Mardi Gras floats. Wonderful? No boring . . . I wanted, expected, intended to get, something better . . . Yes, and I did, I got it. I did things that fat-headed gang never dreamed of. Hell when they were still freshmen at Tulane or LSU or Ole Miss, I sang in the chorus of the biggest show in New York, in *Oklahoma,* and had pictures in *LIFE* in a cowboy outfit, tossin' a ten-gallon hat in the air! YIP . . . EEEEEE! Ha-ha. . . . And at the same time pursued my other vocation. . . . Maybe the only one I was truly meant for, love-making . . . slept in the social register of New York! Millionaires' widows and wives and debutante daughters of such famous names as Vanderbrook and Masters and Halloway and Connaught, names mentioned daily in columns, whose credit cards are their faces. . . . And . . .

PRINCESS: What did they pay you?

CHANCE: I gave people more than I took. Middle-aged people I gave back a feeling of youth. Lonely girls? Understanding, appreciation! An absolutely convincing show of affection. Sad people, lost people? Something light and uplifting! Eccentrics? Tolerance, even odd things they long for. . . . But always just at the point when I might get something back that would solve my own need, which was great, to rise to their level, the memory of my girl would pull me back home to her . . . and when I came home for those visits, man oh man how that town buzzed with excitement. I'm telling you, it would blaze with it, and then that thing in Korea came along. I was about to be sucked into the Army so I went into the Navy, because a sailor's uniform suited me better, the uniform was all that suited me, though. . . .

PRINCESS: Ah-ha!

CHANCE [*mocking her*]: Ah-ha. I wasn't able to stand the goddam routine, discipline. . . . I kept thinking, this stops everything. I was twenty-three, that was the peak of my youth and I knew my youth wouldn't last long. By the time I got out, Christ knows, I might be nearly thirty! Who would remember Chance Wayne? In a life like mine, you just can't stop, you know, can't take time out between steps, you've got to keep going right on up from one thing to the other, once you drop out, it leaves you and goes on without you and you're washed up.

PRINCESS: I don't think I know what you're talking about.

CHANCE: I'm talking about the parade. THE parade! The parade! the boys that go places that's the parade I'm talking about, not a parade of swabbies on a wet deck. And so I ran my comb through my hair one morning and noticed that eight or ten hairs had come out, a warning signal of a future baldness. My hair was still thick. But would it be five years from now, or even three? When the war would be over, that scared me, that speculation. I started to have bad dreams. Nightmares and cold sweats at night, and I had palpitations, and on my leaves I got drunk and woke up in strange places with faces on the next pillow I had never seen before. My eyes had a wild look in them in the mirror. . . . I got the idea I wouldn't live through the war, that I wouldn't come back, that all the excitement and glory of being Chance Wayne would go up in smoke at the moment of contact between my brain and a bit of hot steel that happened to be in the air at the same time and place that my head was . . . that thought didn't comfort me any. Imagine a whole lifetime of dreams and ambitions and hopes dissolving away in one instant, being blacked out like some arithmetic problem washed off a blackboard by a wet sponge, just by some little accident like a bullet, not even aimed at you but just shot off in space, and so I cracked up, my nerves did. I got a medical discharge out of the service and I came home in civvies, then it was when I noticed how different it was, the town and the people in it. Polite? Yes, but not cordial. No headlines in the papers, just an item that measured one inch at the bottom of page five saying that Chance Wayne, the son of Mrs. Emily Wayne of North Front Street, had received an honorable discharge from the Navy as the result of illness and was home to recover . . . that was when Heavenly became more important to me than anything else. . . .

PRINCESS: Is Heavenly a girl's name?

CHANCE: Heavenly is the name of my girl in St. Cloud.

PRINCESS: Is Heavenly why we stopped here?

CHANCE: What other reason for stopping here can you think of?

PRINCESS: So . . . I'm being used. Why not? Even a dead race horse is used to make glue. Is she pretty?

CHANCE [*handing Princess a snapshot*]: This is a flashlight photo I took of her, nude, one night on Diamond Key, which is a little sandbar about half a mile off shore which is under water at high tide. This was taken with the tide coming in. The water is just beginning to lap over her body like it desired her like I did and still do and will always, always. [*Chance takes back the snapshot.*] Heavenly was her name. You can see that it fits her. This was her at fifteen.

PRINCESS: Did you have her that early?

CHANCE: I was just two years older, we had each other that early.

PRINCESS: Sheer luck!

CHANCE: Princess, the great difference between people in this world is not between the rich and the poor or the good and the evil, the biggest of all differences in this world is between the ones that had or have pleasure in love and those that haven't and hadn't any pleasure in love, but just watched it with envy, sick envy. The spectators and the performers. I don't mean just ordinary pleasure or the kind you can buy, I mean great pleasure, and nothing that's happened to me or to Heavenly since can cancel out the many long nights without sleep when we gave each other such pleasure in love as very few people can look back on in their lives . . .

PRINCESS: No question, go on with your story.

CHANCE: Each time I came back to St. Cloud I had her love to come back to. . . .

PRINCESS: Something permanent in a world of change?

CHANCE: Yes, after each disappointment, each failure at something, I'd come back to her like going to a hospital. . . .

PRINCESS: She put cool bandages on your wounds? Why didn't you marry this Heavenly little physician?

CHANCE: Didn't I tell you that Heavenly is the daughter of Boss Finley, the biggest political wheel in this part of the country? Well, if I didn't I made a serious omission.

PRINCESS: He disapproved?

CHANCE: He figured his daughter rated someone a hundred, a thousand per cent better than me, Chance Wayne. . . . The last time I came back here, she phoned me from the drugstore and told me to swim out to Diamond Key, that she would meet me there. I waited a long time, till almost sunset, and the tide started coming in before I heard the put-put of an outboard motor boat coming out to the sandbar. The sun was behind her, I squinted. She had on a silky wet tank suit and fans of water and mist made rainbows about her . . . she stood up in the boat as if she was water-skiing, shouting things at me an' circling around the sandbar, around and around it!

PRINCESS: She didn't come to the sandbar?

CHANCE: No, just circled around it, shouting things at me. I'd swim toward the boat, I would just about reach it and she'd race it away, throwing up misty rainbows, disappearing in rainbows and then circled back and shouting things at me again. . . .

PRINCESS: What things?

CHANCE: Things like, "Chance, go away," "Don't come back to St. Cloud." "Chance, you're a liar." "Chance, I'm sick of your lies!" "My father's right about you!" "Chance, you're no good any more." "Chance, stay away from St. Cloud." The last time around the sandbar she shouted nothing, just waved good-by and turned the boat back to shore.

PRINCESS: Is that the end of the story?

CHANCE: Princess, the end of the story is up to you. You want to help me?

PRINCESS: I want to help you. Believe me, not everybody wants to hurt everybody. I don't want to hurt you, can you believe me?

CHANCE: I can if you prove it to me.

PRINCESS: How can I prove it to you?

CHANCE: I have something in mind.

PRINCESS: Yes, what?

CHANCE: Okay I'll give you a quick outline of this project I have in mind. Soon as I've talked to my girl and shown her my contract, we go on, you and me. Not far, just to New Orleans, Princess. But no more hiding away, we check in at the Hotel Roosevelt there as Alexandra Del Lago and Chance Wayne. Right away the newspapers call you and give a press conference. . . .

PRINCESS: Oh?

CHANCE: Yes! The idea briefly, a local contest of talent to find a pair of young people to star as unknowns in a picture you're planning to make to show your faith in YOUTH, Princess. You stage this contest, you invite other judges, but your decision decides it!

PRINCESS: And you and . . . ?

CHANCE: Yes, Heavenly and I win it. We get her out of St. Cloud, we go to the West Coast together.

PRINCESS: And me?

CHANCE: You?

PRINCESS: Have you forgotten, for instance, that any public attention is what I least want in the world?

CHANCE: What better way can you think of to show the public that you're a person with bigger than personal interest?

PRINCESS: Oh, yes, yes, but not true.

CHANCE: You could pretend it was true.

PRINCESS: If I didn't despise pretending!

CHANCE: I understand. Time does it. Hardens people. Time and the world that you've lived in.

PRINCESS: Which you want for yourself. Isn't that what you want? [*She looks at him then goes to the phone. Into phone.*] Cashier? Hello Cashier? This is the Princess Kosmonopolis speaking. I'm sending down a young man to cash some travelers' checks for me. [*She hangs up.*]

CHANCE: And I want to borrow your Cadillac for a while. . . .

PRINCESS: What for, Chance?

CHANCE [*posturing*]: I'm pretentious. I want to be seen in your car on the streets of St. Cloud. Drive all around town in it, blowing those long silver trumpets and dressed in the fine clothes you bought me. . . . Can I?

PRINCESS: Chance, you're a lost little boy that I really would like to help find himself.

CHANCE: I passed the screen test!

PRINCESS: Come here, kiss me, I love you. [*She faces the audience.*] Did I say that? Did I mean it? [*Then to Chance with arms outstretched.*] What a child you are. . . . Come here. . . . [*He ducks under her arms, and escapes to the chair.*]

CHANCE: I want this big display. Big phony display in your Cadillac around town. And a wad a dough to flash in their faces and the fine clothes you've bought me, on me.

PRINCESS: Did I buy you fine clothes?

CHANCE [*picking up his jacket from the chair*]: The finest. When you stopped being lonely because of my company at that Palm Beach hotel, you bought me the finest. That's the deal for tonight, to toot those silver horns and drive slowly around in the Cadillac convertible so everybody that thought I was washed up will see me. And I have taken my false or true contract to flash in the faces of various people that called me washed up. All right that's the deal. Tomorrow you'll get the car back and what's left of your money. Tonight's all that counts.

PRINCESS: How do you know that as soon as you walk out of this room I won't call the police?

CHANCE: You wouldn't do that, Princess. [*He puts on his jacket.*] You'll find the car in back of the hotel parking lot, and the leftover dough will be in the glove compartment of the car.

PRINCESS: Where will you be?

CHANCE: With my girl, or nowhere.

PRINCESS: Chance Wayne! This was not necessary, all this. I'm not a phony and I wanted to be your friend.

CHANCE: Go back to sleep. As far as I know you're not a bad person, but you just got into bad company on this occasion.

PRINCESS: I am your friend and I'm not a phony. [*Chance turns and goes to the steps.*] When will I see you?

CHANCE [*at the top of the steps*]: I don't know—maybe never.

PRINCESS: Never is a long time, Chance, I'll wait.

[*She throws him a kiss.*]

CHANCE: So long.

[*The Princess stands looking after him as the lights dim and the curtain closes.*]

ACT TWO

SCENE ONE

The terrace of Boss Finley's house, which is a frame house of Victorian Gothic design, suggested by a doorframe at the right and a single white column. As in the other scenes, there are no walls, the action occurring against the sky and sea cyclorama.

The Gulf is suggested by the brightness and the gulls crying as in Act One. There is only essential porch furniture, Victorian wicker but painted bone white. The men should also be wearing white or off-white suits: the tableau is all blue and white, as strict as a canvas of Georgia O'Keeffe's.

At the rise of the curtain, Boss Finley is standing in the center and George Scudder nearby.

BOSS FINLEY: Chance Wayne had my daughter when she was fifteen.

SCUDDER: That young.

BOSS: When she was fifteen he had her. Know how I know? Some flashlight photos were made of her, naked, on Diamond Key.

SCUDDER: By Chance Wayne?

BOSS: My little girl was fifteen, barely out of her childhood when—[*calling offstage*] Charles—

[*Charles enters.*]

BOSS: Call Miss Heavenly—

CHARLES [*concurrently*]: Miss Heavenly. Miss Heavenly. Your daddy wants to see you.

[*Charles leaves.*]

BOSS [*to Scudder*]: By Chance Wayne? Who the hell else do you reckon? I seen them. He had them developed by some studio in Pass Christian that made more copies of them than Chance Wayne ordered and these photos were circulated. I seen them. That was when I first warned the son-of-a-bitch to git and out of St. Cloud. But he's back in St. Cloud right now. I tell you—

SCUDDER: Boss, let me make a suggestion. Call off this rally, I mean your appearance at it, and take it easy tonight. Go out on your boat, you and Heavenly take a short cruise on *The Starfish*. . . .

BOSS: I'm not about to start sparing myself. Oh, I know, I'll have me a coronary and go like that. But not because Chance Wayne had the unbelievable gall to come back to St. Cloud. [*Calling offstage.*] Tom Junior!

TOM JUNIOR [*offstage*]: Yes, sir!

BOSS: Has he checked out yet?

TOM JUNIOR [*entering*]: Hatcher says he called their room at the Royal Palms, and Chance Wayne answered the phone, and Hatcher says . . .

BOSS: Hatcher says—who's Hatcher?

TOM JUNIOR: Dan Hatcher.

BOSS: I hate to expose my ignorance like this but the name Dan Hatcher has no more meaning to me than the name of Hatcher, which is none whatsoever.

SCUDDER [*quietly, deferentially*]: Hatcher, Dan Hatcher, is the assistant manager of the Royal Palms Hotel, and the man that informed me this morning that Chance Wayne was back in St. Cloud.

BOSS: Is this Hatcher a talker, or can he keep his mouth shut?

SCUDDER: I think I impressed him how important it is to handle this thing discreetly.

BOSS: Discreetly, like you handled that operation you done on my daughter, so discreetly that a hillbilly heckler is shouting me questions about it wherever I speak?

SCUDDER: I went to fantastic lengths to preserve the secrecy of that operation.

TOM JUNIOR: When Papa's upset he hits out at anyone near him.

BOSS: I just want to know—has Wayne left?

TOM JUNIOR: Hatcher says that Chance Wayne told him that this old movie star that he's latched on to . . .

SCUDDER: Alexandra Del Lago.

TOM JUNIOR: She's not well enough to travel.

BOSS: Okay, you're a doctor, remove her to a hospital. Call an ambulance and haul her out of the Royal Palms Hotel.

SCUDDER: Without her consent?

BOSS: Say she's got something contagious, typhoid, bubonic plague. Haul her out and slap a quarantine on her hospital door. That way you can separate them. We can remove Chance Wayne from St. Cloud as soon as this Miss Del Lago is removed from Chance Wayne.

SCUDDER: I'm not so sure that's the right way to go about it.

BOSS: Okay, you think of a way. My daughter's no whore, but she had a whore's operation after the last time he had her. I don't want him passin' another night in St. Cloud. Tom Junior.

TOM JUNIOR: Yes, sir.

BOSS: I want him gone by tomorrow—tomorrow commences at midnight.

TOM JUNIOR: I know what to do, Papa. Can I use the boat?

BOSS: Don't ask me, don't tell me nothin'—

TOM JUNIOR: Can I have *The Starfish* tonight?

BOSS: I don't want to know how, just go about it. Where's your sister?

[*Charles appears on the gallery, points out Heavenly lying on the beach to Boss and exits.*]

TOM JUNIOR: She's lyin' out on the beach like a dead body washed up on it.

BOSS [*calling*]: Heavenly!

TOM JUNIOR: Gawge, I want you with me on this boat trip tonight, Gawge.

BOSS [*calling*]: Heavenly!

SCUDDER: I know what you mean, Tom Junior, but I couldn't be involved in it. I can't even know about it.

BOSS [*calling again*]: Heavenly!

TOM JUNIOR: Okay, don't be involved in it. There's a pretty fair doctor that lost his license for helping a girl out of trouble, and he won't be so goddam finicky about doing this absolutely just thing.

SCUDDER: I don't question the moral justification, which is complete without question. . . .

TOM JUNIOR: Yeah, complete without question.

SCUDDER: But I am a reputable doctor, I haven't lost my license. I'm chief of staff at the great hospital put up by your father. . . .

TOM JUNIOR: I said, don't know about it.

SCUDDER: No, sir, I won't know about it . . . [*Boss starts to cough.*] I can't afford to, and neither can your father. . . . [*Scudder goes to gallery writing prescription.*]

BOSS: Heavenly! Come up here, sugar. [*To Scudder.*] What's that you're writing?

SCUDDER: Prescription for that cough.

BOSS: Tear it up, throw it away. I've hawked and spit all my life, and I'll be hawking and spitting in the hereafter. You all can count on that.

[*Auto horn is heard.*]

TOM JUNIOR [*leaps up on the gallery and starts to leave*]: Papa, he's drivin' back by.

BOSS: Tom Junior.

[*Tom Junior stops.*]

TOM JUNIOR: Is Chance Wayne insane?

SCUDDER: Is a criminal degenerate sane or insane is a question that lots of law courts haven't been able to settle.

BOSS: Take it to the Supreme Court, they'll hand you down a decision on that question. They'll tell you a handsome young criminal degenerate like Chance Wayne is the mental and moral equal of any white man in the country.

TOM JUNIOR: He's stopped at the foot of the drive.

BOSS: Don't move, don't move, Tom Junior.

TOM JUNIOR: I'm not movin', Papa.

CHANCE [*offstage*]: Aunt Nonnie! Hey, Aunt Nonnie!

BOSS: What's he shouting?

TOM JUNIOR: He's shouting at Aunt Nonnie.

BOSS: Where is she?

TOM JUNIOR: Runnin' up the drive like a dog-track rabbit.

BOSS: He ain't followin', is he?

TOM JUNIOR: Nope. He's drove away.

[*Aunt Nonnie appears before the veranda, terribly flustered, rooting in her purse for something, apparently blind to the men on the veranda.*]

BOSS: Whatcha lookin' for, Nonnie?

NONNIE [*stopping short*]: Oh—I didn't notice you, Tom. I was looking for my *door* key.

BOSS: Door's open, Nonnie, it's wide open, like a church door.

NONNIE [*laughing*]: Oh, ha, ha . . .

BOSS: Why didn't you answer that good-lookin' boy in the Cadillac car that shouted at you, Nonnie?

NONNIE: Oh. I hoped you hadn't seen him. [*Draws a deep breath and comes on to the terrace, closing her white purse.*] That was Chance Wayne. He's back in St. Cloud, he's at the Royal Palms, he's—

BOSS: Why did you snub him like that? After all these years of devotion?

NONNIE: I went to the Royal Palms to warn him not to stay here but—

BOSS: He was out showing off in that big white Cadillac with the trumpet horns on it.

NONNIE: I left a message for him, I—

TOM JUNIOR: What was the message, Aunt Nonnie? Love and kisses?

NONNIE: Just get out of St. Cloud right away, Chance.

TOM JUNIOR: He's gonna git out, but not in that fishtail Caddy.

NONNIE [*to Tom Junior*]: I hope you don't mean violence— [*turning to Boss*] does he, Tom? Violence don't solve problems. It never solves young people's problems. If you will leave it to me, I'll get him out of St. Cloud. I can, I will, I promise. I don't think Heavenly knows he's back in St. Cloud. Tom, you know, Heavenly says it wasn't Chance that—she says it wasn't Chance.

BOSS: You're like your dead sister, Nonnie, gullible as my wife was. You don't know a lie if you bump into it on a street in the daytime. Now go out there and tell Heavenly I want to see her.

NONNIE: Tom, she's not well enough to—

BOSS: Nonnie, you got a whole lot to answer for.

NONNIE: Have I?

BOSS: Yes, you sure have, Nonnie. You favored Chance Wayne, encouraged, aided and abetted him in his corruption of Heavenly over a long, long time. You go get her. You sure do have a lot to answer for. You got a helluva lot to answer for.

NONNIE: I remember when Chance was the finest, nicest, sweetest boy in St. Cloud, and he stayed that way till you, till you—

BOSS: Go get her, go get her! [*She leaves by the far side of the terrace. After a moment her voice is heard calling, "Heavenly? Heav-*

enly?"] It's a curious thing, a mighty peculiar thing, how often a man that rises to high public office is drug back down by every soul he harbors under his roof. He harbors them under his roof, and they pull the roof down on him. Every last living one of them.

TOM JUNIOR: Does that include me, Papa?

BOSS: If the shoe fits, put it on you.

TOM JUNIOR: How does that shoe fit me?

BOSS: If it pinches your foot, just slit it down the sides a little—it'll feel comfortable on you.

TOM JUNIOR: Papa, you are UNJUST.

BOSS: What do you want credit for?

TOM JUNIOR: I have devoted the past year to organizin' the "Youth for Tom Finley" clubs.

BOSS: I'm carryin' Tom Finley Junior on my ticket.

TOM JUNIOR: You're lucky to have me on it.

BOSS: How do you figure I'm lucky to have you on it?

TOM JUNIOR: I got more newspaper coverage in the last six months than . . .

BOSS: Once for drunk drivin', once for a stag party you thrown in Capitol City that cost me five thousand dollars to hush it up!

TOM JUNIOR: You are so unjust, it . . .

BOSS: And everyone knows you had to be drove through school like a blazeface mule pullin' a plow uphill: flunked out of college with grades that only a moron would have an excuse for.

TOM JUNIOR: I got readmitted to college.

BOSS: At my insistence. By fake examinations, answers provided beforehand, stuck in your fancy pockets. And your promiscuity. Why, these Youth for Tom Finley clubs are practically nothin' but gangs of juvenile delinquents, wearin' badges with my name and my photograph on them.

TOM JUNIOR: How about your well-known promiscuity, Papa? How about your Miss Lucy?

BOSS: Who is Miss Lucy?

TOM JUNIOR [*laughing so hard he staggers*]: Who is Miss Lucy? You don't even know who she is, this woman you keep in a fifty-dollar-a-day hotel suite at the Royal Palms, Papa?

BOSS: What're you talkin' about?

TOM JUNIOR: That rides down the Gulf Stream Highway with a motorcycle escort blowin' their sirens like the Queen of Sheba was going into New Orleans for the day. To use her charge accounts there. And you ask who's Miss Lucy? She don't even talk good of you. She says you're too old for a lover.

BOSS: That is a goddam lie. Who says Miss Lucy says that?

TOM JUNIOR: She wrote it with lipstick on the ladies' room mirror at the Royal Palms.

BOSS: Wrote what?

TOM JUNIOR: I'll quote it to you exactly. "Boss Finley," she wrote, "is too old to cut the mustard."

[*Pause: the two stags, the old and the young one, face each other, panting. Scudder has discreetly withdrawn to a far end of porch.*]

BOSS: I don't believe this story!

TOM JUNIOR: Don't believe it.

BOSS: I will check on it, however.

TOM JUNIOR: I already checked on it. Papa, why don't you get rid of her, huh, Papa?

[*Boss Finley turns away, wounded, baffled: stares out at the audience with his old, bloodshot eyes as if he thought that someone out there had shouted a question at him which he didn't quite hear.*]

BOSS: Mind your own goddam business. A man with a mission, which he holds sacred, and on the strength of which he rises to high public office—crucified in this way, publicly, by his own offspring.

[*Heavenly has entered on the gallery.*] Ah, here she is, here's my little girl. [*Stopping Heavenly.*] You stay here, honey. I think you all had better leave me alone with Heavenly now, huh—yeah. . . . [*Tom Junior and Scudder exit.*] Now, honey, you stay here. I want to have a talk with you.

HEAVENLY: Papa, I can't talk now.

BOSS: It's necessary.

HEAVENLY: I can't, I can't talk now.

BOSS: All right, don't talk, just listen.

[*But she doesn't want to listen, starts away: He would have restrained her forcibly if an old colored manservant, Charles, had not, at that moment, come out on the porch. He carries a stick, a hat, a package, wrapped as a present. Puts them on a table.*]

CHARLES: It's five o'clock, Mister Finley.

BOSS: Huh? Oh—thanks . . .

[*Charles turns on a coach lamp by the door. This marks a formal division in the scene. The light change is not realistic; the light doesn't seem to come from the coach lamp but from a spectral radiance in the sky, flooding the terrace.*

The sea wind sings. Heavenly lifts her face to it. Later that night may be stormy, but now there is just a quickness and freshness coming in from the Gulf. Heavenly is always looking that way, toward the Gulf, so that the light from Point Lookout catches her face with its repeated soft stroke of clarity.

In her father, a sudden dignity is revived. Looking at his very beautiful daughter, he becomes almost stately. He approaches her, soon as the colored man returns inside, like an aged courtier comes deferentially up to a crown princess or infanta. It's important not to think of his attitude toward her in the terms of crudely conscious incestuous feeling, but just in the natural terms of almost any aging father's feeling for a beautiful young daughter who reminds him of a dead wife that he desired intensely when she was the age of his daughter.

At this point there might be a phrase of stately, Mozartian music, suggesting a court dance. The flagged terrace may suggest the parquet floor of a ballroom and the two players' movements may suggest the stately, formal movements of a court dance of that time; but if this effect is used, it should be just a suggestion. The change toward "stylization" ought to be held in check.]

BOSS: You're still a beautiful girl.

HEAVENLY: Am I, Papa?

BOSS: Of course you are. Lookin' at you nobody could guess that—

HEAVENLY [*laughs*]: The embalmers must have done a good job on me, Papa. . . .

BOSS: You got to quit talkin' like that. [*Then, seeing Charles.*] Will you get back in the house! [*Phone rings.*]

CHARLES: Yes, sir, I was just—

BOSS: Go on in! If that phone call is for me, I'm in only to the governor of the state and the president of the Tidewater Oil Corporation.

CHARLES [*offstage*]: It's for Miss Heavenly again.

BOSS: Say she ain't in.

CHARLES: Sorry, she ain't in.

[*Heavenly has moved upstage to the low parapet or sea wall that separates the courtyard and lawn from the beach. It is early dusk. The coach lamp has cast a strange light on the setting, which is neoromantic: Heavenly stops by an ornamental urn containing a tall fern that the salty Gulf wind has stripped nearly bare. The Boss follows her, baffled.*]

BOSS: Honey, you say and do things in the presence of people as if you had no regard of the fact that people have ears to hear you and tongues to repeat what they hear. And so you become a issue.

HEAVENLY: Become what, Papa?

BOSS: A issue, a issue, subject of talk, of scandal—which can defeat the mission that—

HEAVENLY: Don't give me your Voice of God speech. Papa, there was a time when you could have saved me, by letting me marry a boy that was still young and clean, but instead you drove him away, drove him out of St. Cloud. And when he came back, you took me out of St. Cloud, and tried to force me to marry a fifty-year-old money bag that you wanted something out of—

BOSS: Now, honey—

HEAVENLY: —and then another, another, all of them ones that you wanted something out of. I'd gone, so Chance went away. Tried to compete, make himself big as these big shots you wanted to use me for a bond with. He went. He tried. The right doors wouldn't open, and so he went in the wrong ones, and—Papa, you married for love, why wouldn't you let me do it, while I was alive, inside, and the boy still clean, still decent?

BOSS: Are you reproaching me for—?

HEAVENLY [*shouting*]: Yes, I am, Papa, I am. You married for love, but you wouldn't let me do it, and even though you'd done it, you broke Mama's heart, Miss Lucy had been your mistress—

BOSS: Who is Miss Lucy?

HEAVENLY: Oh, Papa, she was your mistress long before Mama died. And Mama was just a front for you. Can I go in now, Papa? Can I go in now?

BOSS: No, no, not till I'm through with you. What a terrible, terrible thing for my baby to say . . . [*He takes her in his arms.*] Tomorrow, tomorrow morning, when the big after-Easter sales commence in the stores—I'm gonna send you in town with a motorcycle escort, straight to the Maison Blanche. When you arrive at the store, I want you to go directly up to the office of Mr. Harvey C. Petrie and tell him to give you unlimited credit there. Then go down and outfit yourself as if you was—buyin' a trousseau to marry the Prince of Monaco. . . . Purchase a full wardrobe, includin' furs. Keep 'em in storage until winter. Gown? Three, four, five, the most lavish. Slippers? Hell, pairs and pairs of 'em. Not one hat—but a dozen. I made a pile of dough on a deal involvin' the sale of rights to oil under water here lately, and baby, I want you to buy a piece of jewelry. Now about that, you better tell Harvey to call me. Or better still, maybe Miss Lucy had better help you select it. She's wise as a backhouse rat when it comes to a stone,—that's for sure. . . . Now where'd I buy that clip that I give your mama? D'you remember the clip I bought your mama? Last thing I give your mama before she died . . . I knowed she was dyin' when I bought her that clip, and I bought that clip for fifteen thousand dollars mainly to make her think she was going to get well. . . . When I pinned it on her on the nightgown she was wearing, that poor thing started crying. She said, for God's sake, Boss, what does a dying woman want with such a big diamond? I said to her, honey, look at the price tag on it. What does the price tag say? See them five figures, that one and that five and them three aughts on there? Now, honey, make sense, I told her. If you was dying, if there was any chance of it, would I invest fifteen grand in a diamond clip to pin on the neck of a shroud? Ha, haha. That made the old lady laugh. And she sat up as bright as a little bird in that bed with the diamond clip on, receiving callers all day, and laughing and chatting with them, with that diamond clip on inside and she died before midnight, with that diamond clip on her. And not till the very last minute did she believe that the diamonds wasn't a proof that she wasn't dying. [*He moves to terrace, takes off robe and starts to put on tuxedo coat.*]

HEAVENLY: Did you bury her with it?

BOSS: Bury her with it? Hell, no. I took it back to the jewelry store in the morning.

HEAVENLY: Then it didn't cost you fifteen grand after all.

BOSS: Hell, did I care what it cost me? I'm not a small man. I wouldn't have cared one hoot if it cost me a million . . . if at that time I had that kind of loot in my pockets. It would have been worth that money to see that one little smile your mama bird give me at noon of the day she was dying.

HEAVENLY: I guess that shows, demonstrates very clearly, that you have got a pretty big heart after all.

BOSS: Who doubts it then? Who? Who ever? [*He laughs.*]

[*Heavenly starts to laugh and then screams hysterically. She starts going toward the house. Boss throws down his cane and grabs her.*]

Just a minute, Missy. Stop it. Stop it. Listen to me, I'm gonna tell you something. Last week in New Bethesda, when I was speaking on the threat of desegregation to white women's chastity in the South, some heckler in the crowd shouted out, "Hey, Boss Finley, how about your daughter? How about that operation you had done on your daughter at the Thomas J. Finley hospital in St. Cloud? Did she put on black in mourning for her appendix?" Same heckler, same question when I spoke in the Coliseum at the state capital.

HEAVENLY: What was your answer to him?

BOSS: He was removed from the hall at both places and roughed up a little outside it.

HEAVENLY: Papa, you have got an illusion of power.

BOSS: I have power, which is not an illusion.

HEAVENLY: Papa, I'm sorry my operation has brought this embarrassment on you, but can you imagine it, Papa? I felt worse than embarrassed when I found out that Dr. George Scudder's knife had cut the youth out of my body, made me an old childless woman. Dry, cold, empty, like an old woman. I feel as if I ought to rattle like a dead dried-up vine when the Gulf wind blows, but, Papa—I won't embarrass you any more. I've made up my mind about something. If they'll let me, accept me, I'm going into a convent.

BOSS [*shouting*]: You ain't going into no convent. This state is a Protestant region and a daughter in a convent would politically ruin me. Oh, I know, you took your mama's religion because in your heart you always wished to defy me. Now, tonight, I'm addressing the Youth for Tom Finley clubs in the ballroom of the Royal Palms Hotel. My speech is going out over a national TV network, and Missy, you're going to march in the ballroom on my arm. You're going to be wearing the stainless white of a virgin, with a Youth for Tom Finley button on one shoulder and a corsage of lilies on the other. You're going to be on the speaker's platform with me, you on one side of me and Tom Junior on the other, to scotch these rumors about your corruption. And you're gonna wear a proud happy smile on your face, you're gonna stare straight out at the crowd in the ballroom with pride and joy in your eyes. Lookin' at you, all in white like a virgin, nobody would dare to speak or believe the ugly stories about you. I'm relying a great deal on this campaign to bring in young voters for the crusade I'm leading. I'm all that stands between the South and the black days of Reconstruction. And you and Tom Junior are going to stand there beside me in the grand crystal ballroom, as shining examples of white Southern youth—in danger.

HEAVENLY [*defiant*]: Papa, I'm not going to do it.

BOSS: I didn't say would you, I said you would, and you will.

HEAVENLY: Suppose I still say I won't.

BOSS: Then you won't, that's all. If you won't, you won't. But there would be consequences you might not like. [*Phone rings.*] Chance Wayne is back in St. Cloud.

CHARLES [*offstage*]: Mr. Finley's residence. Miss Heavenly? Sorry, she's not in.

BOSS: I'm going to remove him, he's going to be removed from St. Cloud. How do you want him to leave, in that white Cadillac he's riding around in, or in the scow that totes the garbage out to the dumping place in the Gulf?

HEAVENLY: You wouldn't dare!

BOSS: You want to take a chance on it?

CHARLES [*enters*]: That call was for you again, Miss Heavenly.

BOSS: A lot of people approve of taking violent action against corrupters. And on all of them that want to adulterate the pure white blood of the South. Hell, when I was fifteen, I come down barefoot out of the red clay hills as if the Voice of God called me. Which it did, I believe. I firmly believe He called me. And nothing, nobody, nowhere is gonna stop me, never. . . . [*He motions to Charles for gift. Charles hands it to him.*] Thank you, Charles. I'm gonna pay me an early call on Miss Lucy.

[*A sad, uncertain note has come into his voice on this final line. He turns and plods wearily, doggedly off at left.*]

THE CURTAIN FALLS

[*House remains dark for short intermission.*]

SCENE TWO

A corner of cocktail lounge and of outside gallery of the Royal Palms Hotel. This corresponds in style to the bedroom set: Victorian with Moorish influence. Royal palms are projected on the cyclorama which is deep violet with dusk. There are Moorish arches between gallery and interior: over the single table, inside, is suspended the same lamp, stained glass and ornately wrought metal, that hung in the bedroom. Perhaps on the gallery there is a low stone balustrade that supports, where steps descend into the garden, an electric light standard with five branches and pear-shaped globes of a dim pearly luster. Somewhere out of the sight-lines an entertainer plays a piano or novachord.

The interior table is occupied by two couples that represent society in St. Cloud. They are contemporaries of Chance's. Behind the bar is Stuff who feels the dignity of his recent advancement from drugstore soda fountain to the Royal Palms cocktail lounge: he has on a white mess jacket, a scarlet cummerbund and light blue trousers, flatteringly close-fitted. Chance Wayne was once barman here: Stuff moves with an indolent male grace that he may have unconsciously remembered admiring in Chance.

Boss Finley's mistress, Miss Lucy, enters the cocktail lounge dressed in a ball gown elaborately ruffled and very bouffant like an antebellum Southern belle's. A single blonde curl is arranged to switch girlishly at one side of her sharp little terrier face. She is outraged over something and her glare is concentrated on Stuff who "plays it cool" behind the bar.

STUFF: Ev'nin', Miss Lucy.

MISS LUCY: I wasn't allowed to sit at the banquet table. No. I was put at a little side table, with a couple of state legislators an' wives. [*She sweeps behind the bar in a proprietary fashion.*] Where's your Grant's twelve-year-old? Hey! Do you have a big mouth? I used to remember a kid that jerked sodas at Walgreen's that had a big mouth. . . . Put some ice in this. . . . Is yours big, huh? I want to tell you something.

STUFF: What's the matter with your finger?

[*She catches him by his scarlet cummerbund.*]

MISS LUCY: I'm going to tell you just now. The boss came over to me with a big candy Easter egg for me. The top of the egg unscrewed. He told me to unscrew it. So I unscrewed it. Inside was a little blue velvet jewel box, no not little, a big one, as big as somebody's mouth, too.

STUFF: Whose mouth?

MISS LUCY: The mouth of somebody who's not a hundred miles from here.

STUFF [*going off at the left*]: I got to set my chairs. [*Stuff re-enters at once carrying two chairs. Sets them at tables while Miss Lucy talks.*]

MISS LUCY: I open the jewel box an' start to remove the great big diamond clip in it. I just got my fingers on it, and start to remove it and the old son of a bitch slams the lid of the box on my fingers. One fingernail is still blue. And the boss says to me, "Now go downstairs to the cocktail lounge and go in the ladies' room and describe this diamond clip with lipstick on the ladies' room mirror down there. Hanh?—and he put the jewel box in his pocket and slammed the door so hard goin' out of my suite that a picture fell off the wall.

STUFF [*setting the chairs at the table*]: Miss Lucy, you are the one that said, "I wish you would see what's written with lipstick on the ladies' room mirror" las' Saturday night.

MISS LUCY: To you! Because I thought I could trust you.

STUFF: Other people were here an' all of them heard it.

MISS LUCY: Nobody but you at the bar belonged to the Youth for Boss Finley Club.

[*Both stop short. They've noticed a tall man who has entered the cocktail lounge. He has the length and leanness and luminous pallor of a face that El Greco gave to his saints. He has a small bandage near the hairline. His clothes are country.*]

Hey, you.

HECKLER: Evenin', ma'am.

MISS LUCY: You with the Hillbilly Ramblers? You with the band?

HECKLER: I'm a hillbilly, but I'm not with no band.

[*He notices Miss Lucy's steady, interested stare. Stuff leaves with a tray of drinks.*]

MISS LUCY: What do you want here?

HECKLER: I come to hear Boss Finley talk. [*His voice is clear but strained. He rubs his large Adam's apple as he speaks.*]

MISS LUCY: You can't get in the ballroom without a jacket and a tie on. . . . I know who you are. You're the heckler, aren't you?

HECKLER: I don't heckle. I just ask questions, one question or two or three questions, depending on how much time it takes them to grab me and throw me out of the hall.

MISS LUCY: Those questions are loaded questions. You gonna repeat them tonight?

HECKLER: Yes, ma'am, if I can get in the ballroom, and make myself heard.

MISS LUCY: What's wrong with your voice?

HECKLER: When I shouted my questions in New Bethesda last week I got hit in the Adam's apple with the butt of a pistol, and that affected my voice. It still ain't good, but it's better. [*Starts to go.*]

MISS LUCY [*goes to back of bar, where she gets jacket, the kind kept in places with dress regulations, and throws it to Heckler*]: Wait. Here, put this on. The Boss's talking on a national TV hookup tonight. There's a tie in the pocket. You sit perfectly still at the bar till the Boss starts speaking. Keep your face back of this *Evening Banner.* O.K.?

HECKLER [*opening the paper in front of his face*]: I thank you.

MISS LUCY: I thank you, too, and I wish you more luck than you're likely to have.

[*Stuff re-enters and goes to back of the bar.*]

FLY [*entering on the gallery*]: Paging Chance Wayne. [*Auto horn offstage.*] Mr. Chance Wayne, please. Paging Chance Wayne. [*He leaves.*]

MISS LUCY [*to Stuff who has re-entered*]: Is Chance Wayne back in St. Cloud?

STUFF: You remember Alexandra Del Lago?

MISS LUCY: I guess I do. I was president of her local fan club. Why?

CHANCE [*offstage*]: Hey, boy, park that car up front and don't wrinkle them fenders.

STUFF: She and Chance Wayne checked in here last night.

MISS LUCY: Well I'll be a dawg's mother. I'm going to look into that. [*Lucy exits.*]

CHANCE [*entering and crossing to the bar*]: Hey, Stuff! [*He takes a cocktail off the bar and sips it.*]

STUFF: Put that down. This ain't no cocktail party.

CHANCE: Man, don't you know . . . phew . . . nobody drinks gin martinis with olives. Everybody drinks vodka martinis with lemon twist nowadays, except the squares in St. Cloud. When I had your job, when I was the barman here at the Royal Palms, I created that uniform you've got on. . . . I copied it from an outfit Vic Mature wore in a Foreign Legion picture, and I looked better in it than he did, and almost as good in it as you do, ha, ha. . . .

AUNT NONNIE [*who has entered at the right*]: Chance. Chance . . .

CHANCE: Aunt Nonnie! [*to Stuff*]: Hey, I want a tablecloth on that table, and a bucket of champagne . . . Mumm's Cordon Rouge. . . .

AUNT NONNIE: You come out here.

CHANCE: But, I just ordered champagne in here. [*Suddenly his effusive manner collapses, as she stares at him gravely.*]

AUNT NONNIE: I can't be seen talking to you. . . .

[*She leads him to one side of the stage. A light change has occurred which has made it a royal palm grove with a bench. They cross to it solemnly. Stuff busies himself at the bar, which is barely lit. After a moment he exits with a few drinks to main body of the cocktail lounge off left. Bar music. "Quiereme Mucho."*]

CHANCE [*following her*]: Why?

AUNT NONNIE: I've got just one thing to tell you, Chance, get out of St. Cloud.

CHANCE: Why does everybody treat me like a low criminal in the town I was born in?

AUNT NONNIE: Ask yourself that question, ask your conscience that question.

CHANCE: What question?

AUNT NONNIE: You know, and I know you know . . .

CHANCE: Know what?

AUNT NONNIE: I'm not going to talk about it. I just can't talk about it. Your head and your tongue run wild. You can't be trusted. We have to live in St. Cloud. . . . Oh, Chance, why have you changed like you've changed? Why do you live on nothing but wild dreams now, and have no address where anybody can reach you in time to—reach you?

CHANCE: Wild dreams! Yes. Isn't life a wild dream? I never heard a better description of it. . . . [*He takes a pill and a swallow from a flask.*]

AUNT NONNIE: What did you just take, Chance? You took something out of your pocket and washed it down with liquor.

CHANCE: Yes, I took a wild dream and—washed it down with another wild dream, Aunt Nonnie, that's my life now. . . .

AUNT NONNIE: Why, son?

CHANCE: Oh, Aunt Nonnie, for God's sake, have you forgotten what was expected of me?

AUNT NONNIE: People that loved you expected just one thing of you—sweetness and honesty and . . .

[*Stuff leaves with tray.*]

CHANCE [*kneeling at her side*]: No, not after the brilliant beginning I made. Why, at seventeen, I put on, directed, and played the leading role in *The Valiant,* that one-act play that won the state drama contest. Heavenly played in it with me, and have you forgotten? You went with us as the girls' chaperone to the national contest held in . . .

AUNT NONNIE: Son, of course I remember.

CHANCE: In the parlor car? How we sang together?

AUNT NONNIE: You were in love even then.

CHANCE: God, yes, we were in love! [*He sings softly.*]

"If you like-a me, like I like-a you,

And we like-a both the same"

TOGETHER:

"I'd like-a say, this very day,

I'd like-a change your name."

[*Chance laughs softly, wildly, in the cool light of the palm grove. Aunt Nonnie rises abruptly. Chance catches her hands.*]

AUNT NONNIE: You—*do*—take unfair advantage. . . .

CHANCE: Aunt Nonnie, we didn't win that lousy national contest, we just placed second.

AUNT NONNIE: Chance, you didn't place second. You got honorable mention. Fourth place, except it was just called honorable mention.

CHANCE: Just honorable mention. But in a national contest, honorable mention means something. . . . We would have won it, but I blew my lines. Yes, I that put on and produced the damn thing, couldn't even hear the damn lines being hissed at me by that fat girl with the book in the wings. [*He buries his face in his hands.*]

AUNT NONNIE: I loved you for that, son, and so did Heavenly, too.

CHANCE: It was on the way home in the train that she and I. . . .

AUNT NONNIE [*with a flurry of feeling*]: I know, I— I—

CHANCE [*rising*]: I bribed the Pullman conductor to let us use for an hour a vacant compartment on that sad, home-going train—

AUNT NONNIE: I know, I— I—

CHANCE: Gave him five dollars, but that wasn't enough, and so I gave him my wrist watch, and my collar pin and tie clip and signet ring and my suit, that I'd bought on credit to go to the contest. First suit I'd ever put on that cost more than thirty dollars.

AUNT NONNIE: Don't go back over that.

CHANCE: —To buy the first hour of love that we had together. When she undressed, I saw that her body was just then, barely, beginning to be a woman's and . . .

AUNT NONNIE: Stop, Chance.

CHANCE: I said, oh, Heavenly, no, but she said yes, and I cried in her arms that night, and didn't know that what I was crying for was—youth, that would go.

AUNT NONNIE: It was from that time on, you've changed.

CHANCE: I swore in my heart that I'd never again come in second in any contest, especially not now that Heavenly was my—Aunt Nonnie, look at this contract. [*He snatches out papers and lights lighter.*]

AUNT NONNIE: I don't want to see false papers.

CHANCE: These are genuine papers. Look at the notary's seal and the signatures of the three witnesses on them. Aunt Nonnie, do you know who I'm with? I'm with Alexandra Del Lago, the Princess Kosmonopolis is my—

AUNT NONNIE: Is your what?

CHANCE: Patroness! Agent! Producer! She hasn't been seen much lately, but still has influence, power, and money—money that can open all doors. That I've knocked at all these years till my knuckles are bloody.

AUNT NONNIE: Chance, even now, if you came back here simply saying, "I couldn't remember the lines, I lost the contest, I—failed," but you've come back here again with—

CHANCE: Will you just listen one minute more? Aunt Nonnie, here is the plan. A local-contest-of-Beauty.

AUNT NONNIE: Oh, Chance.

CHANCE: A local contest of talent that she will win.

AUNT NONNIE: Who?

CHANCE: Heavenly.

AUNT NONNIE: No, Chance. She's not young now, she's faded, she's . . .

CHANCE: Nothing goes that quick, not even youth.

AUNT NONNIE: Yes, it does.

CHANCE: It will come back like magic. Soon as I . . .

AUNT NONNIE: For what? For a fake contest?

CHANCE: For love. The moment I hold her.

AUNT NONNIE: Chance.

CHANCE: It's not going to be a local thing, Aunt Nonnie. It's going to get national coverage. The Princess Kosmonopolis's best friend is that sob sister, Sally Powers. Even you know Sally Powers. Most powerful movie columnist in the world. Whose name is law in the motion . . .

AUNT NONNIE: Chance, lower your voice.

CHANCE: I want people to hear me.

AUNT NONNIE: No, you don't, no you don't. Because if your voice gets to Boss Finley, you'll be in great danger, Chance.

CHANCE: I go back to Heavenly, or I don't. I live or die. There's nothing in between for me.

AUNT NONNIE: What you want to go back to is your clean, unashamed youth. And you can't.

CHANCE: You still don't believe me, Aunt Nonnie?

AUNT NONNIE: No, I don't. Please go. Go away from here, Chance.

CHANCE: Please.

AUNT NONNIE: No, no, go away!

CHANCE: Where to? Where can I go? This is the home of my heart. Don't make me homeless.

AUNT NONNIE: Oh, Chance.

CHANCE: Aunt Nonnie. Please.

AUNT NONNIE [*rises and starts to go*]: I'll write to you. Send me an address. I'll write to you.

[*She exits through bar. Stuff enters and moves to bar.*]

CHANCE: Aunt Nonnie . . .

[*She's gone*]

[*Chance removes a pint bottle of vodka from his pocket and something else which he washes down with the vodka. He stands back as two couples come up the steps and cross the gallery into the bar: they sit at a table. Chance takes a deep breath. Fly enters lighted area inside, singing out "Paging Mr. Chance Wayne, Mr. Chance Wayne, pagin' Mr. Chance Wayne."—Turns about smartly and goes back out through lobby. The name has stirred a commotion at the bar and table visible inside.*]

EDNA: Did you hear *that?* Is *Chance Wayne* back in St. Cloud?

[*Chance draws a deep breath. Then, he stalks back into the main part of the cocktail lounge like a matador entering a bull ring.*]

VIOLET: My God, yes—there he is.

[*Chance reads Fly's message.*]

CHANCE [*to Fly*]: Not now, later, later.

[*The entertainer off left begins to play a piano . . . The "evening" in the cocktail lounge is just beginning.*]

[*Fly leaves through the gallery.*]

Well! Same old place, same old gang. Time doesn't pass in St. Cloud. [*To Bud and Scotty*] Hi!

BUD: How are you . . .

CHANCE [*shouting offstage*]: Hey, Jackie . . . [*Fly enters and stands on terrace. Piano stops. Chance crosses over to the table that holds the foursome.*] . . . remember my song? Do you—remember my song? . . . You see, he remembers my song. [*The entertainer swings into "It's a Big Wide Wonderful World."*] Now I feel at home. In my home town . . . Come on, everybody—sing!

[*This token of apparent acceptance reassures him. The foursome at the table on stage studiously ignore him. He sings:*]

"When you're in love you're a master
Of all you survey, you're a gay Santa Claus.
There's a great big star-spangled sky up above you,
When you're in love you're a hero . . ."

Come on! Sing, ev'rybody!

[*In the old days they did; now they don't. He goes on, singing a bit; then his voice dies out on a note of embarrassment. Somebody at the bar whispers something and another laughs. Chance chuckles uneasily and says:*]

What's wrong here? The place is dead.

STUFF: You been away too long, Chance.

CHANCE: Is that the trouble?

STUFF: That's all. . . .

[*Jackie, off, finishes with an arpeggio. The piano slams. There is a curious hush in the bar. Chance looks at the table. Violet whispers something to Bud. Both girls rise abruptly and cross out of the bar.*]

BUD [*yelling at Stuff*]: Check, Stuff.

CHANCE [*with exaggerated surprise*]: Well, *Bud and Scotty.* I didn't see you at all. Wasn't that Violet and Edna at your table? [*He sits at the table between Bud and Scotty.*]

SCOTTY: I guess they didn't recognize you, Chance.

BUD: Violet did.

SCOTTY: Did Violet?

BUD: She said, "My God, Chance Wayne."

SCOTTY: That's recognition and profanity, too.

CHANCE: I don't mind. I've been snubbed by experts, and I've done some snubbing myself. . . . Hey! [*Miss Lucy has entered at left. Chance sees her and goes toward her.*] —Is that Miss Lucy or is that Scarlett O'Hara?

MISS LUCY: Hello there, Chance Wayne. Somebody said that you were back in St. Cloud, but I didn't believe them. I said I'd have to see it with my own eyes before . . . Usually there's an item in the paper, in Gwen Phillips's column saying "St. Cloud youth home on visit is slated to play featured role in important new picture," and me being a movie fan I'm always thrilled by it. . . . [*She ruffles his hair.*]

CHANCE: Never do that to a man with thinning hair. [*Chance's smile is unflinching; it gets harder and brighter.*]

MISS LUCY: Is your hair thinning, baby? Maybe that's the difference I noticed in your appearance. Don't go 'way till I get back with my drink. . . .

[*She goes to back of bar to mix herself a drink. Meanwhile, Chance combs his hair.*]

SCOTTY [*to Chance*]: Don't throw away those golden hairs you combed out, Chance. Save 'em and send 'em each in letters to your fan clubs.

BUD: Does Chance Wayne have a fan club?

SCOTTY: The most patient one in the world. They've been waiting years for him to show up on the screen for more than five seconds in a crowd scene.

MISS LUCY [*returning to the table*]: Y'know this boy Chance Wayne used to be so attractive I couldn't stand it. But now I can, almost stand it. Every Sunday in summer I used to drive out to the municipal beach and watch him dive off the high tower. I'd take binoculars with me when he put on those free divin' exhibitions. You still dive, Chance? Or have you given that up?

CHANCE [*uneasily*]: I did some diving last Sunday.

MISS LUCY: Good, as ever?

CHANCE: I was a little off form, but the crowd didn't notice. I can still get away with a double back somersault and a—

MISS LUCY: Where was this, in Palm Beach, Florida, Chance?

[*Hatcher enters.*]

CHANCE [*stiffening*]: Why Palm Beach? Why there?

MISS LUCY: Who was it said they seen you last month in Palm Beach? Oh yes, Hatcher—that you had a job as a beach-boy at some big hotel there?

HATCHER [*stops at steps of the terrace, then leaves across the gallery*]: Yeah, that's what I heard.

CHANCE: Had a job—as a beach-boy?

STUFF: Rubbing oil into big fat millionaires.

CHANCE: What joker thought up that one? [*His laugh is a little too loud.*]

SCOTTY: You ought to get their names and sue them for slander.

CHANCE: I long ago gave up tracking down sources of rumors about me. Of course, it's flattering, it's gratifying to know that you're still being talked about in your old home town, even if what they say is completely fantastic. Hahaha.

[*Entertainer returns, sweeps into "Quiereme Mucho."*]

MISS LUCY: Baby, you've changed in some way, but I can't put my finger on it. You all see a change in him, or has he just gotten older? [*She sits down next to Chance.*]

CHANCE [*quickly*]: To change is to live, Miss Lucy, to live is to change, and not to change is to die. You know that, don't you? It used to scare me sometimes. I'm not scared of it now. Are you scared of it, Miss Lucy? Does it scare you?

[*Behind Chance's back one of the girls has appeared and signaled the boys to join them outside. Scotty nods and holds up two fingers to mean they'll come in a couple of minutes. The girl goes back out with an angry head-toss.*]

SCOTTY: Chance, did you know Boss Finley was holding a Youth for Tom Finley rally upstairs tonight?

CHANCE: I saw the announcements of it all over town.

BUD: He's going to state his position on that emasculation business that's stirred up such a mess in the state. Had you heard about that?

CHANCE: No.

SCOTTY: He must have been up in some earth satellite if he hasn't heard about that.

CHANCE: No, just out of St. Cloud.

SCOTTY: Well, they picked out a nigger at random and castrated the bastard to show they mean business about white women's protection in this state.

BUD: Some people think they went too far about it. There's been a whole lot of Northern agitation all over the country.

SCOTTY: The Boss is going to state his own position about that thing before the Youth for Boss Finley rally upstairs in the Crystal Ballroom.

CHANCE: Aw. Tonight?

STUFF: Yeah, t'night.

BUD: They say that Heavenly Finley and Tom Junior are going to be standing on the platform with him.

PAGEBOY [*entering*]: Paging Chance Wayne. Paging . . .

[*He is stopped short by Edna.*]

CHANCE: I *doubt* that story, somehow I *doubt* that story.

STUFF: You doubt they cut that nigger?

CHANCE: Oh, no, that I don't doubt. You know what that is, don't you? Sex-envy is what that is, and the revenge for sex-envy which is a widespread disease that I have run into personally too often for me to doubt its existence or any manifestation. [*The group push back their chairs, snubbing him. Chance takes the message from the Page-boy, reads it and throws it on the floor.*] Hey, Stuff!—What d'ya have to do, stand on your head to get a drink around here?—Later, tell her.—Miss Lucy, can you get that Walgreen's soda jerk to give me a shot of vodka on the rocks? [*She snaps her fingers at Stuff. He shrugs and sloshes some vodka onto ice.*]

MISS LUCY: Chance? You're too loud, baby.

CHANCE: Not loud enough, Miss Lucy. No. What I meant that I doubt is that Heavenly Finley, that only I know in St. Cloud, would stoop to stand on a platform next to her father while he explains and excuses on TV this random emasculation of a young Nigra caught on a street after midnight. [*Chance is speaking with an almost incoherent excitement, one knee resting on the seat of his chair, swaying the chair back and forth. The Heckler lowers his newspaper from his face; a slow fierce smile spreads over his face as he leans forward with tensed throat muscles to catch Chance's burst of oratory.*] No! That's what I do not believe. If I believed it, oh, I'd give you a diving exhibition. I'd dive off municipal pier and swim straight out to Diamond Key and past it, and keep on swimming till sharks and barracuda took me for live bait, brother. [*His chair topples over backward, and he sprawls to the floor. The Heckler springs up to catch him. Miss Lucy springs up too, and sweeps between Chance and the Heckler, pushing the Heckler back with a quick, warning look or gesture. Nobody notices the Heckler. Chance scrambles back to his feet, flushed, laughing. Bud and Scotty outlaugh him. Chance picks up his chair and continues. The laughter stops.*] Because I have come back to St. Cloud to take her out of St. Cloud. Where I'll take her is not to a place anywhere except to her place in my heart. [*He has removed a pink capsule from his pocket, quickly and furtively, and drunk it down with his vodka.*]

BUD: Chance, what did you swallow just now?

CHANCE: Some hundred-proof vodka.

BUD: You washed something down with it that you took out of your pocket.

SCOTTY: It looked like a little pink pill.

CHANCE: Oh, ha ha. Yes, I washed down a goof-ball. You want one? I got a bunch of them. I always carry them with me. When you're not having fun, it makes you have it. When you're having fun, it makes you have more of it. Have one and see.

SCOTTY: Don't that damage the brain?

CHANCE: No, the contrary. It stimulates the brain cells.

SCOTTY: Don't it make your eyes look different, Chance?

MISS LUCY: Maybe that's what I noticed, [*as if wishing to change the subject*] Chance, I wish you'd settle an argument for me.

CHANCE: What argument, Miss Lucy?

MISS LUCY: About who you're traveling with. I heard you checked in here with a famous old movie star.

[*They all stare at him. . . . In a way he now has what he wants. He's the center of attraction: everybody is looking at him, even though with hostility, suspicion and a cruel sense of sport.*]

CHANCE: Miss Lucy I'm traveling with the vice-president and major stockholder of the film studio which just signed me.

MISS LUCY: Wasn't she once in the movies and very well known?

CHANCE: She was and still is and never will cease to be an important, a legendary figure in the picture industry, here and all over the world, and I am now under personal contract to her.

MISS LUCY: What's her name, Chance?

CHANCE: She doesn't want her name known. Like all great figures, world-known, she doesn't want or need and refuses to have the wrong type of attention. Privacy is a luxury to great stars. Don't ask me her name. I respect her too much to speak her name at this table. I'm obligated to her because she has shown faith in me. It took a long hard time to find that sort of faith in my talent that this woman has shown me. And I refuse to betray it at this table. [*His voice rises; he is already "high."*]

MISS LUCY: Baby, why are you sweating and your hands shaking so? You're not sick, are you?

CHANCE: Sick? Who's sick? I'm the least sick one you know.

MISS LUCY: Well, baby, you know you oughtn't to stay in St. Cloud. Y'know that, don't you? I couldn't believe my ears when I heard you were back here. [*to the two boys*] Could you all believe he was back here?

SCOTTY: What did you come back for?

CHANCE: I wish you would give me one reason why I shouldn't come back to visit the grave of my mother and pick out a monument for her, and share my happiness with a girl that I've loved many years. It's her, Heavenly Finley, that I've fought my way up for, and now that I've made it, the glory will be hers, too. And I've just about persuaded the powers to be to let her appear with me in a picture I'm signed for. Because I . . .

BUD: What is the name of this picture?

CHANCE: . . . Name of it? "Youth!"

BUD: Just "Youth?"

CHANCE: Isn't that a great title for a picture introducing young talent? You all look doubtful. If you don't believe me, well, look. Look at this contract. [*Removes it from his pocket.*]

SCOTTY: You carry the contract with you?

CHANCE: I happen to have it in this jacket pocket.

MISS LUCY: Leaving, Scotty? [*Scotty has risen from the table.*]

SCOTTY: It's getting too deep at this table.

BUD: The girls are waiting.

CHANCE [*quickly*]: Gee, Bud, that's a clean set of rags you're wearing, but let me give you a tip for your tailor. A guy of medium stature looks better with natural shoulders, the padding cuts down your height, it broadens your figure and gives you a sort of squat look.

BUD: Thanks, Chance.

SCOTTY: You got any helpful hints for my tailor, Chance?

CHANCE: Scotty, there's no tailor on earth that can disguise a sedentary occupation.

MISS LUCY: Chance, baby . . .

CHANCE: You still work down at the bank? You sit on your can all day countin' century notes and once every week they let you slip one in your pockets? That's a fine setup, Scotty, if you're satisfied with it but it's starting to give you a little pot and a can.

VIOLET [*appears in the door, angry*]: Bud! Scotty! Come on.

SCOTTY: I don't get by on my looks, but I drive my own car. It isn't a Caddy, but it's my own car. And if my own mother died, I'd bury her myself; I wouldn't let a church take up a collection to do it.

VIOLET [*impatiently*]: Scotty, if you all don't come now I'm going home in a taxi.

[*The two boys follow her into the Palm Garden. There they can be seen giving their wives cab money, and indicating they are staying.*]

CHANCE: The squares have left us, Miss Lucy.

MISS LUCY: Yeah.

CHANCE: Well . . . I didn't come back here to fight with old friends of mine. . . . Well, it's quarter past seven.

MISS LUCY: Is it?

[*There are a number of men, now, sitting around in the darker corners of the bar, looking at him. They are not ominous in their attitudes. They are simply waiting for something, for the meeting to start upstairs, for something. . . . Miss Lucy stares at Chance and the men, then again at Chance, nearsightedly, her head cocked like a puzzled terrier's. Chance is discomfited.*]

CHANCE: Yep . . . How is that Hickory Hollow for steaks? Is it still the best place in town for a steak?

STUFF [*answering the phone at the bar*]: Yeah, it's him. He's here. [*Looks at Chance ever so briefly, hangs up.*]

MISS LUCY: Baby, I'll go to the checkroom and pick up my wrap and call for my car and I'll drive you out to the airport. They've got an air-taxi out there, a whirly-bird taxi, a helicopter, you know, that'll hop you to New Orleans in fifteen minutes.

CHANCE: I'm not leaving St. Cloud. What did I say to make you think I was?

MISS LUCY: I thought you had sense enough to know that you'd better.

CHANCE: Miss Lucy, you've been drinking, it's gone to your sweet little head.

MISS LUCY: Think it over while I'm getting my wrap. You still got a friend in St. Cloud.

CHANCE: I still have a girl in St. Cloud, and I'm not leaving without her.

PAGEBOY [*offstage*]: Paging Chance Wayne, Mr. Chance Wayne, please.

PRINCESS [*entering with Pageboy*]: Louder, young man, louder . . . Oh, never mind, here he is!

[*But Chance has already rushed out onto the gallery. The Princess looks as if she had thrown on her clothes to escape a building on fire. Her blue-sequined gown is unzipped, or partially zipped, her hair is disheveled, her eyes have a dazed, drugged brightness; she is holding up the eyeglasses with the broken lens, shakily, hanging onto her mink stole with the other hand; her movements are unsteady.*]

MISS LUCY: I know who you are. Alexandra Del Lago.

[*Loud whispering. A pause.*]

PRINCESS [*on the step to the gallery*]: What? Chance!

MISS LUCY: Honey, let me fix that zipper for you. Hold still just a second. Honey, let me take you upstairs. You mustn't be seen down here in this condition. . . .

[*Chance suddenly rushes in from the gallery: he conducts the Princess outside: she is on the verge of panic. The Princess rushes half down the steps to the palm garden: leans panting on the stone balustrade under the ornamental light standard with its five great pearls of light. The interior is dimmed as Chance comes out behind her.*]

PRINCESS: Chance! Chance! Chance! Chance!

CHANCE [*softly*]: If you'd stayed upstairs that wouldn't have happened to you.

PRINCESS: I did, I stayed.

CHANCE: I told you to wait.

PRINCESS: I waited.

CHANCE: Didn't I tell you to wait till I got back?

PRINCESS: I did, I waited forever, I waited forever for you. Then finally I heard those long sad silver trumpets blowing through the Palm Garden and then—Chance, the most wonderful thing has happened to me. Will you listen to me? Will you let me tell you?

MISS LUCY [*to the group at the bar*]: Shhh!

PRINCESS: Chance, when I saw you driving under the window with your head held high, with that terrible stiff-necked pride of the defeated which I know so well; I knew that your comeback had been a failure like mine. And I felt something in my heart for you. That's a miracle, Chance. That's the wonderful thing that happened to me. I felt something for someone besides myself. That means my heart's still alive, at least some part of it is, not all of my heart is dead yet. Part's alive still. . . . Chance, please listen to me. I'm ashamed of this morning. I'll never degrade you again, I'll never degrade myself, you and me, again by—I wasn't always this monster. Once I wasn't this monster. And what I felt in my heart when I saw you returning, defeated, to this palm garden, Chance, gave me hope that I could stop being a monster. Chance, you've got to help me stop being the monster that I was this morning, and you can do it, can help me. I won't be ungrateful for it. I almost died this morning, suffocated in a panic. But even through my panic, I saw your kindness. I saw a true kindness in you that you have almost destroyed, but that's still there, a little. . . .

CHANCE: What kind thing did I do?

PRINCESS: You gave my oxygen to me.

CHANCE: Anyone would do that.

PRINCESS: It could have taken you longer to give it to me.

CHANCE: I'm not that kind of monster.

PRINCESS: You're no kind of monster. You're just—

CHANCE: What?

PRINCESS: Lost in the beanstalk country, the ogre's country at the top of the beanstalk, the country of the flesh-hungry, blood-thirsty ogre—

[*Suddenly a voice is heard from off.*]

VOICE: Wayne?

[*The call is distinct but not loud. Chance hears it, but doesn't turn toward it; he freezes momentarily, like a stag scenting hunters. Among the people gathered inside in the cocktail lounge we see the speaker, Dan Hatcher. In appearance, dress and manner he is the apotheosis of the assistant hotel manager, about Chance's age, thin, blond-haired, trim blond mustache, suave, boyish, betraying an instinct for murder only by the ruby-glass studs in his matching cuff links and tie clip.*]

HATCHER: Wayne!

[*He steps forward a little and at the same instant Tom Junior and Scotty appear behind him, just in view. Scotty strikes a match for Tom Junior's cigarette as they wait there. Chance suddenly gives the Princess his complete and tender attention, putting an arm around her and turning her toward the Moorish arch to the bar entrance.*]

CHANCE [*loudly*]: I'll get you a drink, and then I'll take you upstairs. You're not well enough to stay down here.

HATCHER [*crossing quickly to the foot of the stairs*]: Wayne!

[*The call is too loud to ignore: Chance half turns and calls back.*]

CHANCE: Who's that?

HATCHER: Step down here a minute!

CHANCE: Oh, *Hatcher!* I'll be right with you.

PRINCESS: Chance, don't leave me alone.

[*At this moment the arrival of Boss Finley is heralded by the sirens of several squad cars. The forestage is suddenly brightened from off left, presumably the floodlights of the cars arriving at the entrance to the hotel. This is the signal the men at the bar have been waiting for. Everybody rushes off left. In the hot light all alone on stage is Chance; behind him, is the Princess. And the Heckler is at the bar. The entertainer plays a feverish tango. Now, off left, Boss Finley can be heard, his public personality very much "on." Amid the flash of flash bulbs we hear off:*]

BOSS [*off*]: Hahaha! Little Bit, smile! Go on, smile for the birdie! Ain't she Heavenly, ain't that the right name for her!

HEAVENLY [*off*]: Papa, I want to go in!

[*At this instant she runs in—to face Chance. . . . The Heckler rises. For a long instant, Chance and Heavenly stand there: he on the steps leading to the Palm Garden and gallery; she in the cocktail lounge. They simply look at each other . . . the Heckler between them. Then the Boss comes in and seizes her by the arm. . . . And there he is facing the Heckler and Chance both. . . . For a split second he faces them, half lifts his cane to strike at them, but doesn't strike . . . then pulls Heavenly back off left stage . . . where the photographing and interviews proceed during what follows. Chance has seen that Heavenly is going to go on the platform with her father. . . . He stands there stunned. . . .*]

PRINCESS: Chance! Chance? [*He turns to her blindly*] Call the car and let's go. Everything's packed, even the . . . tape recorder with my shameless voice on it. . . .

[*The Heckler has returned to his position at the bar. Now Hatcher and Scotty and a couple of other of the boys have come out. . . . The Princess sees them and is silent. . . . She's never been in anything like this before. . . .*]

HATCHER: Wayne, step down here, will you.

CHANCE: What for, what do you want?

HATCHER: Come down here, I'll tell you.

CHANCE: You come up here and tell me.

TOM JUNIOR: Come on, you chicken-gut bastard.

CHANCE: Why, hello, Tom Junior. Why are you hiding down there?

TOM JUNIOR: You're hiding, not me, chicken-gut.

CHANCE: You're in the dark, not me.

HATCHER: Tom Junior wants to talk to you privately down here.

CHANCE: He can talk to me privately up here.

TOM JUNIOR: Hatcher, tell him I'll talk to him in the washroom on the mezzanine floor.

CHANCE: I don't hold conversations with people in washrooms. . . .

[*Tom Junior infuriated, starts to rush forward. Men restrain him.*]

What is all this anyhow? It's fantastic. You all having a little conference there? I used to leave places when I was told to. Not now. That time's over. Now I leave when I'm ready. Hear that, Tom Junior? Give your father that message. This is my town. I was born in St. Cloud, not him. He was just called here. He was just called down from the hills to preach hate. I was born here to make love. Tell him about that difference between him and me, and ask him which he thinks has more right to stay here. . . . [*He gets no answer from the huddled little group which is restraining Tom Junior from perpetrating murder right there in the cocktail lounge. After all, that would be a bad incident to precede the Boss's all-South-wide TV appearance . . . and they all know it. Chance, at the same time, continues to taunt them.*] Tom, Tom Junior! What do you want me for? To pay me back for the ball game and picture show money I gave you when you were cutting your father's yard grass for a dollar on Saturday? Thank me for the times I gave you my motorcycle and got you a girl to ride the buddy seat with you? Come here! I'll give you the keys to my Caddy. I'll give you the price of any whore in St. Cloud. You still got credit with me because you're Heavenly's brother.

TOM JUNIOR [*almost bursting free*]: Don't say the name of my sister!

CHANCE: I said the name of my girl!

TOM JUNIOR [*breaking away from the group*]: I'm all right, I'm all right. Leave us alone, will you. I don't want Chance to feel that he's outnumbered. [*He herds them out.*] O.K.? Come on down here.

PRINCESS [*trying to restrain Chance*]: No, Chance, don't.

TOM JUNIOR: Excuse yourself from the lady and come on down here. Don't be scared to. I just want to talk to you quietly. Just talk. Quiet talk.

CHANCE: Tom Junior, I know that since the last time I was here something has happened to Heavenly and I—

TOM JUNIOR: Don't—speak the name of my sister. Just leave her name off your tongue—

CHANCE: Just tell me what happened to her.

TOM JUNIOR: Keep your ruttin' voice down.

CHANCE: I know I've done many wrong things in my life, many more than I can name or number, but I swear I never hurt Heavenly in my life.

TOM JUNIOR: You mean to say my sister was had by somebody else—diseased by somebody else the last time you were in St. Cloud? . . . I know, it's possible, it's barely possible that you didn't know what you done to my little sister the last time you come to St.

Cloud. You remember that time when you came home broke? My sister had to pick up your tabs in restaurants and bars, and had to cover bad checks you wrote on banks where you had no accounts. Until you met this rich bitch, Minnie, the Texas one with the yacht, and started spending week ends on her yacht, and coming back Mondays with money from Minnie to go on with my sister. I mean, you'd sleep with Minnie, that slept with any goddam gigolo bastard she could pick up on Bourbon Street or the docks, and then you would go on sleeping again with my sister. And sometime, during that time, you got something besides your gigolo fee from Minnie and passed it onto my sister, my little sister that had hardly even heard of a thing like that, and didn't know what it was till it had gone on too long and—

CHANCE: I left town before I found out I—

[*"The Lamentation" is heard.*]

TOM JUNIOR: You found out! Did you tell my little sister?

CHANCE: I thought if something was wrong she'd write me or call me—

TOM JUNIOR: How could she write you or call you, there're no addresses, no phone numbers in gutters. I'm itching to kill you—here, on this spot! . . . My little sister, Heavenly, didn't know about the diseases and operations of whores, till she had to be cleaned and cured—I mean spayed like a dawg by Dr. George Scudder's knife. That's right—by the knife! . . . And tonight—if you stay here tonight, if you're here after this rally, you're gonna get the knife, too. You know? The knife? That's all. Now go on back to the lady, I'm going back to my father. [*Tom Junior exits.*]

PRINCESS [*as Chance returns to her*]: Chance, for God's sake, let's go now . . .

[*"The Lament" is in the air. It blends with the wind-blown sound of the palms.*]

All day I've kept hearing a sort of lament that drifts through the air of this place. It says, "Lost, lost, never to be found again." Palm gardens by the sea and olive groves on Mediterranean islands all have that lament drifting through them. "Lost, lost". . . . The isle of Cyprus,

Monte Carlo, San Remo, Torremolenas, Tangiers. They're all places of exile from whatever we loved. Dark glasses, wide-brimmed hats and whispers, "Is that her?" Shocked whispers. . . . Oh, Chance, believe me, after failure comes flight. Nothing ever comes after failure but flight. Face it. Call the car, have them bring down the luggage and let's go on along the Old Spanish Trail. [*She tries to hold him.*]

CHANCE: Keep your grabbing hands off me.

[*Marchers offstage start to sing "Bonnie Blue Flag."*]

PRINCESS: There's no one but me to hold you back from destruction in this place.

CHANCE: I don't want to be held.

PRINCESS: Don't leave me. If you do I'll turn into the monster again. I'll be the first lady of the Beanstalk Country.

CHANCE: Go back to the room.

PRINCESS: I'm going nowhere alone. I can't.

CHANCE [*in desperation*]: Wheel chair! [*Marchers enter from the left, Tom Junior and Boss with them.*] Wheel chair! Stuff, get the lady a wheel chair! She's having another attack!

[*Stuff and a Bellboy catch at her . . . but she pushes Chance away and stares at him reproachfully. . . . The Bellboy takes her by the arm. She accepts this anonymous arm and exits. Chance and the Heckler are alone on stage.*]

CHANCE [*as if reassuring, comforting somebody besides himself*]: It's all right, I'm alone now, nobody's hanging onto me.

[*He is panting. Loosens his tie and collar. Band in the Crystal Ballroom, muted, strikes up a lively but lyrically distorted variation of some such popular tune as the "Liechtensteiner Polka." Chance turns toward the sound. Then, from left stage, comes a drum majorette, bearing a gold and purple silk banner inscribed, "Youth For Tom Finley," prancing and followed by Boss Finley, Heavenly and Tom Junior, with a tight grip on her arm, as if he were conducting her to a death chamber.*]

TOM JUNIOR: Papa? Papa! Will you tell Sister to march?

BOSS FINLEY: Little Bit, you hold your haid up *high* when we march into that ballroom. [*Music up high . . . They march up the steps and onto the gallery in the rear . . . then start across it. The Boss calling out:*] Now march! [*And they disappear up the stairs.*]

VOICE [*offstage*]: Now let us pray. [*There is a prayer mumbled by many voices.*]

MISS LUCY [*who has remained behind*]: You still want to try it?

HECKLER: I'm going to take a shot at it. How's my voice?

MISS LUCY: Better.

HECKLER: I better wait here till he starts talkin', huh?

MISS LUCY: Wait till they turn down the chandeliers in the ballroom. . . . Why don't you switch to a question that won't hurt his daughter?

HECKLER: I don't want to hurt his daughter. But he's going to hold her up as the fair white virgin exposed to black lust in the South, and that's his build-up, his lead into his Voice of God speech.

MISS LUCY: He honestly believes it.

HECKLER: I don't believe it. I believe that the silence of God, the absolute speechlessness of Him is a long, long and awful thing that the whole world is lost because of. I think it's yet to be broken to any man, living or any yet lived on earth—no exceptions, and least of all Boss Finley.

[*Stuff enters, goes to table, starts to wipe it. The chandelier lights go down.*]

MISS LUCY [*with admiration*]: It takes a hillbilly to cut down a hillbilly. . . . [*to Stuff*] Turn on the television, baby.

VOICE [*offstage*]: I give you the beloved Thomas J. Finley.

[*Stuff makes a gesture as if to turn on the TV, which we play in the fourth wall. A wavering beam of light, flickering, narrow, intense, comes from the balcony rail. Stuff moves his head so that he's in it, looking into it. . . . Chance walks slowly downstage, his head also in the narrow flickering beam of light. As he walks downstage, there suddenly appears on the big TV screen, which is the whole back wall of the stage, the image of Boss Finley. His arm is around Heavenly and he is speaking. . . . When Chance sees the Boss's arm around Heavenly, he makes a noise in his throat like a hard fist hit him low. . . . Now the sound, which always follows the picture by an instant, comes on . . . loud.*]

BOSS [*on TV screen*]: Thank you, my friends, neighbors, kinfolk, fellow Americans. . . . I have told you before, but I will tell you again. I got a mission that I hold sacred to perform in the Southland. . . . When I was fifteen I came down barefooted out of the red clay hills. . . . Why? Because the Voice of God called me to execute this mission.

MISS LUCY [*to Stuff*]: He's too loud.

HECKLER: Listen!

BOSS: And what is this mission? I have told you before but I will tell you again. To shield from pollution a blood that I think is not only sacred to me, but sacred to Him.

[*Upstage we see the Heckler step up the last steps and make a gesture as if he were throwing doors open. . . . He advances into the hall, out of our sight.*]

MISS LUCY: Turn it down, Stuff.

STUFF [*motioning to her*]: Shh!

BOSS: Who is the colored man's best friend in the South? That's right . . .

MISS LUCY: Stuff, turn down the volume.

BOSS: It's me, Tom Finley. So recognized by both races.

STUFF [*shouting*]: He's speaking the word. Pour it on!

BOSS: However—I can't and will not accept, tolerate, condone this threat of a blood pollution.

[*Miss Lucy turns down the volume of the TV set.*]

BOSS: As you all know I had no part in a certain operation on a young black gentleman. I call that incident a deplorable thing. That is the one thing about which I am in total agreement with the Northern radical press. It was a de-plorable thing. However . . . I understand the emotions that lay behind it. The passion to protect by this violent emotion something that we hold sacred: our purity of our own blood! But I had no part in, and I did not condone the operation performed on the unfortunate colored gentleman caught prowling the midnight streets of our Capitol City. . . .

CHANCE: Christ! What lies. What a liar!

MISS LUCY: Wait! . . . Chance, you can still go. I can still help you, baby.

CHANCE [*putting hands on Miss Lucy's shoulders*]: Thanks, but no thank you, Miss Lucy. Tonight, God help me, somehow, I don't know how, but somehow I'll take her out of St. Cloud. I'll wake her up in my arms, and I'll give her life back to her. Yes, somehow, God help me, somehow!

[*Stuff turns up volume of TV set.*]

HECKLER [*as voice on the TV*]: Hey, Boss Finley! [*The TV camera swings to show him at the back of the hall.*] How about your daughter's operation? How about that operation your daughter had done on her at the Thomas J. Finley hospital here in St. Cloud? Did she put on black in mourning for her appendix? . . .

[*We hear a gasp, as if the Heckler had been hit. Picture: Heavenly horrified. Sounds of a disturbance. Then the doors at the top stairs up left burst open and the Heckler tumbles down. . . . The picture changes to Boss Finley. He is trying to dominate the disturbance in the hall.*]

BOSS: Will you repeat that question. Have that man step forward. I will answer his question. Where is he? Have that man step forward, I will answer his question. . . . Last Friday . . . Last Friday, Good Friday. I said last Friday, Good Friday . . . Quiet, may I have your attention please. . . . Last Friday, Good Friday, I seen a horrible thing on the campus of our great State University, which I built for the state. A hideous straw-stuffed effigy of myself, Tom Finley, was hung and set fire to in the main quadrangle of the college. This outrage was inspired . . . inspired by the Northern radical press. However, that was Good Friday. Today is Easter. I saw that was Good Friday. Today is Easter Sunday and I am in St. Cloud.

[*During this a gruesome, not-lighted, silent struggle has been going on. The Heckler defended himself, but finally has been overwhelmed and rather systematically beaten. . . . The tight intense follow spot beam stayed on Chance. If he had any impulse to go to the Heckler's aid, he'd be discouraged by Stuff and another man who stand behind him, watching him. . . . At the height of the beating, there are bursts of great applause. . . . At a point during it, Heavenly is suddenly escorted down the stairs, sobbing, and collapses. . . .*]

CURTAIN

ACT THREE

A while later that night: the hotel bedroom. The shutters in the Moorish corner are thrown open on the Palm Garden: scattered sounds of disturbance are still heard: something burns in the Palm Garden: an effigy, an emblem? Flickering light from it falls on the Princess. Over the interior scene, the constant serene projection of royal palms, branched among stars.

PRINCESS [*pacing with the phone*]: Operator! What's happened to my driver?

[*Chance enters on the gallery, sees someone approaching on other side—quickly pulls back and stands in shadows on the gallery.*]

You told me you'd get me a driver. . . . Why can't you get me a driver when you said that you would? Somebody in this hotel can surely get me somebody to drive me at any price asked!—out of this infernal . . .

[*She turns suddenly as Dan Hatcher knocks at the corridor door. Behind him appear Tom Junior, Bud and Scotty, sweaty, disheveled from the riot in the Palm Garden.*]

Who's that?

SCOTTY: She ain't gonna open, break it in.

PRINCESS [*dropping phone*]: What do you want?

HATCHER: Miss Del Lago . . .

BUD: Don't answer till she opens.

PRINCESS: Who's out there! What do you want?

SCOTTY [*to shaky Hatcher*]: Tell her you want her out of the goddamn room.

HATCHER [*with forced note of authority*]: Shut up. Let me handle this . . . Miss Del Lago, your check-out time was three-thirty P.M., and it's now after midnight. . . . I'm sorry but you can't hold this room any longer.

PRINCESS [*throwing open the door*]: What did you say? Will you repeat what you said! [*Her imperious voice, jewels, furs and commanding presence abash them for a moment.*]

HATCHER: Miss Del Lago . . .

TOM JUNIOR [*recovering quickest*]: This is Mr. Hatcher, assistant manager here. You checked in last night with a character not wanted here, and we been informed he's stayin' in your room with you. We brought Mr. Hatcher up here to remind you that the check-out time is long past and—

PRINCESS [*powerfully*]: My check-out time at any hotel in the world is *when I want to check out. . . .*

TOM JUNIOR: This ain't any hotel in the world.

PRINCESS [*making no room for entrance*]: Also, I don't talk to assistant managers of hotels when I have complaints to make about discourtesies to me, which I do most certainly have to make about my experiences here. I don't even talk to managers of hotels, I talk to owners of them. Directly to hotel owners about discourtesies to me. [*Picks up satin sheets on bed.*] These sheets are mine, they go with me. And I have never suffered such dreadful discourtesies to me at any hotel at any time or place anywhere in the world. Now I have found out the name of this hotel owner. This is a chain hotel under the ownership of a personal friend of mine whose guest I have been in foreign capitals such as . . . [*Tom Junior has pushed past her into the room.*] What in hell is he doing in my room?

TOM JUNIOR: Where is Chance Wayne?

PRINCESS: Is that what you've come here for? You can go away then. He hasn't been in this room since he left this morning.

TOM JUNIOR: Scotty, check the bathroom. . . . [*He checks a closet, stoops to peer under the bed. Scotty goes off at right.*] Like I told you before, we know you're Alexandra Del Lago traveling with a degenerate that I'm sure you don't know. That's why you can't stay in St. Cloud, especially after this ruckus that we— [*Scotty re-enters from the bathroom and indicates to Tom Junior that Chance is not there.*] —Now if you need any help in getting out of St. Cloud, I'll be—

PRINCESS [*cutting in*]: Yes. I want a driver. Someone to drive my car. I want to leave here. I'm desperate to leave here. I'm not able to drive. I have to be driven away!

TOM JUNIOR: Scotty, you and Hatcher wait outside while I explain something to her. . . . [*They go and wait outside the door, on the left end of the gallery.*] I'm gonna git you a driver, Miss Del Lago. I'll git you a state trooper, half a dozen state troopers if I can't get you no driver. O.K.? Some time come back to our town n' see us, hear? We'll lay out a red carpet for you. O.K.? G'night, Miss Del Lago.

[*They disappear down the hall, which is then dimmed out. Chance now turns from where he's been waiting at the other end of the corridor and slowly, cautiously, approaches the entrance to the room. Wind sweeps the Palm Garden; it seems to dissolve the walks; the rest of the play is acted against the night sky. The shuttered doors on the veranda open and Chance enters the room. He has gone a good deal further across the border of reason since we last saw him. The Princess isn't aware of his entrance until he slams the shuttered doors. She turns, startled, to face him.*]

PRINCESS: Chance!

CHANCE: You had some company here.

PRINCESS: Some men were here looking for you. They told me I wasn't welcome in this hotel and this town because I had come here with "a criminal degenerate." I asked them to get me a driver so I can go.

CHANCE: I'm your driver. I'm still your driver, Princess.

PRINCESS: You couldn't drive through the Palm Garden.

CHANCE: I'll be all right in a minute.

PRINCESS: It takes more than a minute, Chance, will you listen to me? Can you listen to me? I listened to you this morning, with understanding and pity, I did, I listened with pity to your story this morning. I felt something in my heart for you which I thought I couldn't feel. I remembered young men who were what you are or what you're hoping to be. I saw them all clearly, all clearly, eyes, voices, smiles, bodies clearly. But their names wouldn't come back to me. I couldn't get their names back without digging into old programs of plays that I starred in at twenty in which they said, "Madam, the Count's waiting for you," or—Chance? They almost made it. Oh, oh, Franz! Yes, Franz . . . what? Albertzart. Franz Albertzart, oh God, God, Franz Albertzart . . . I had to fire him. He held me too tight in the waltz scene, his anxious fingers left bruises once so violent, they, they dislocated a disc in my spine, and—

CHANCE: I'm waiting for you to shut up.

PRINCESS: I saw him in Monte Carlo not too long ago. He was with a woman of seventy, and his eyes looked older than hers. She held him, she led him by an invisible chain through Grand Hotel . . . lobbies and casinos and bars like a blind, dying lap dog; he wasn't much older than you are now. Not long after that he drove his Alfa-Romeo or Ferrari off the Grand Corniche—accidentally?—broke his skull like an eggshell. I wonder what they found in it? Old, despaired-of ambitions, little treacheries, possibly even little attempts at blackmail that didn't quite come off, and whatever traces are left of really great charm and sweetness. Chance, Franz Albertzart is Chance Wayne. Will you please try to face it so we can go on together?

CHANCE [*pulls away from her*]: Are you through? Have you finished?

PRINCESS: You didn't listen, did you?

CHANCE [*picking up the phone*]: I didn't have to. I told you that story this morning—I'm not going to drive off nothing and crack my head like an eggshell.

PRINCESS: No, because you can't drive.

CHANCE: Operator? Long distance.

PRINCESS: You would drive into a palm tree. Franz Albertzart . . .

CHANCE: Where's your address book, your book of telephone numbers?

PRINCESS: I don't know what you think that you are up to, but it's no good. The only hope for you now is to let me lead you by that invisible loving steel chain through Carltons and Ritzes and Grand Hotels and—

CHANCE: Don't you know, I'd die first? I would rather die first . . . [*into phone*] Operator? This is an urgent person-to-person call from Miss Alexandra Del Lago to Miss Sally Powers in Beverly Hills, California. . . .

PRINCESS: Oh, no! . . . Chance!

CHANCE: Miss Sally Powers, the Hollywood columnist, yes, Sally Powers. Yes, well get information. I'll wait, I'll wait. . . .

PRINCESS: Her number is Coldwater five-nine thousand. . . . [*Her hand goes to her mouth—but too late.*]

CHANCE: In Beverly Hills, California, Coldwater five-nine thousand.

[*The Princess moves out onto forestage; surrounding areas dim till nothing is clear behind her but the Palm Garden.*]

PRINCESS: Why did I give him the number? Well, why not, after all, I'd have to know sooner or later . . . I started to call several times, picked up the phone, put it down again. Well, let him do it for me. Something's happened. I'm breathing freely and deeply as if the panic was over. Maybe it's over. He's doing the dreadful thing for me, asking the answer for me. He doesn't exist for me now except as somebody making this awful call for me, asking the answer for me. The light's on me. He's almost invisible now. What does that mean? Does it mean that I still wasn't ready to be washed up, counted out?

CHANCE: All right, call Chasen's. Try to reach her at Chasen's.

PRINCESS: Well, one thing's sure. It's only this call I care for. I seem to be standing in light with everything else dimmed out. He's in the dimmed-out background as if he'd never left the obscurity he was born in. I've taken the light again as a crown on my head to which I am suited by something in the cells of my blood and body from the time of my birth. It's mine, I was born to own it, as he was born to make this phone call for me to Sally Powers, dear faithful custodian of my outlived legend. [*Phone rings in distance.*] The legend that I've outlived. . . . Monsters don't die early; they hang on long. Awfully long. Their vanity's infinite, almost as infinite as their disgust with themselves. . . . [*Phone rings louder: it brings the stage light back up on the hotel bedroom. She turns to Chance and the play returns to a more realistic level.*] The phone's still ringing.

CHANCE: They gave me another number. . . .

PRINCESS: If she isn't there, give my name and ask them where I can reach her.

CHANCE: Princess?

PRINCESS: What?

CHANCE: I have a personal reason for making this phone call.

PRINCESS: I'm quite certain of that.

CHANCE [*into phone*]: I'm calling for Alexandra Del Lago. She wants to speak to Miss Sally Powers— Oh, is there any number where the Princess could reach her?

PRINCESS: It will be a good sign if they give you a number.

CHANCE: Oh?—good, I'll call that number . . . Operator? Try another number for Miss Sally Powers. It's Canyon seven-five thousand . . . Say it's urgent, it's Princess Kosmonopolis . . .

PRINCESS: Alexandra Del Lago.

CHANCE: Alexandra Del Lago is calling Miss Powers.

PRINCESS [*to herself*]: Oxygen, please, a little. . . .

CHANCE: Is that you, Miss Powers? This is Chance Wayne talking . . . I'm calling for the Princess Kosmonopolis, she wants to speak to you. She'll come to the phone in a minute. . . .

PRINCESS: I can't. . . . Say I've . . .

CHANCE [*stretching phone cord*]: This is as far as I can stretch the cord, Princess, you've got to meet it halfway.

[*Princess hesitates; then advances to the extended phone.*]

PRINCESS [*in a low, strident whisper*]: Sally? Sally? Is it really you, Sally? Yes, it's me, Alexandra. It's what's left of me, Sally. Oh, yes, I was there, but I only stayed a few minutes. Soon as they started laughing in the wrong places, I fled up the aisle and into the street screaming Taxi—and never stopped running till now. No, I've talked to nobody, heard nothing, read nothing . . . just wanted—dark . . . What? You're just being kind.

CHANCE [*as if to himself*]: Tell her that you've discovered a pair of new stars. Two of them.

PRINCESS: One moment, Sally, I'm—breathless!

CHANCE [*gripping her arm*]: And lay it on thick. Tell her to break it tomorrow in her column, in all of her columns, and in her radio talks . . . that you've discovered a pair of young people who are the stars of tomorrow!

PRINCESS [*to Chance*]: Go into the bathroom. Stick your head under cold water. . . . Sally . . . Do you really think so? You're not just being nice, Sally, because of old times—Grown, did you say? My talent? In what way, Sally? More depth? More what, did you say? More power!—well, Sally, God bless you, dear Sally.

CHANCE: Cut the chatter. Talk about me and *HEAVENLY!*

PRINCESS: No, of course I didn't read the reviews. I told you I flew, I flew. I flew as fast and fast as I could. Oh. Oh? Oh . . . How very sweet of you, Sally. I don't even care if you're not altogether sincere in that statement, Sally. I think you know what the past fifteen years have been like, because I do have the—"out-crying heart of an—artist." Excuse me, Sally, I'm crying, and I don't have any Kleenex. Excuse me, Sally, I'm crying. . . .

CHANCE [*hissing behind her*]: Hey. Talk about me! [*She kicks Chance's leg.*]

PRINCESS: What's that, Sally? Do you really believe so? Who? For what part? Oh, my God! . . . Oxygen, oxygen, quick!

CHANCE [*seizing her by the hair and hissing*]: Me! Me!—You bitch!

PRINCESS: Sally? I'm too overwhelmed. Can I call you back later? Sally, I'll call back later. . . . [*She drops phone in a daze of rapture.*] My picture has broken box-office records. In New York and L. A.!

CHANCE: Call her back, get her on the phone.

PRINCESS: Broken box-office records. The greatest comeback in the history of the industry, that's what she calls it . . .

CHANCE: You didn't mention me to her.

PRINCESS [*to herself*]: I can't appear, not yet. I'll need a week in a clinic, then a week or ten days at the Morning Star Ranch at Vegas. I'd better get Ackermann down there for a series of shots before I go on to the Coast. . . .

CHANCE [*at phone*]: Come back here, call her again.

PRINCESS: I'll leave the car in New Orleans and go on by plane to, to, to—Tucson. I'd better get Strauss working on publicity for me. I'd better be sure my tracks are covered up well these last few weeks in—hell!—

CHANCE: Here. Here, get her back on this phone.

PRINCESS: Do what?

CHANCE: Talk about me and talk about Heavenly to her.

PRINCESS: Talk about a beach-boy I picked up for pleasure, distraction from panic? Now? When the nightmare is over? Involve my name, which is Alexandra Del Lago, with the record of a— You've just been using me. Using me. When I needed you downstairs you shouted, "Get her a wheel chair!" Well, I didn't need a wheel chair, I came up alone, as always. I climbed back alone up the beanstalk to the ogre's country where I live, now, alone. Chance, you've gone past something you couldn't afford to go past; your time, your youth, you've passed it. It's all you had, and you've had it.

CHANCE: Who in hell's talking! Look. [*He turns her forcibly to the mirror.*] Look in that mirror. What do you see in that mirror?

PRINCESS: I see—Alexandra Del Lago, artist and star! Now it's your turn, you look and what do you see?

CHANCE: I see—Chance Wayne. . . .

PRINCESS: The face of a Franz Albertzart, a face that tomorrow's sun will touch without mercy. Of course, you were crowned with laurel in the beginning, your gold hair was wreathed with laurel, but the gold is thinning and the laurel has withered. Face it—pitiful monster. [*She touches the crown of his head.*] . . . Of course, I know I'm one too. But one with a difference. Do you know what that difference is? No, you don't know. I'll tell you. We are two monsters, but with this difference between us. Out of the passion and torment of my existence I have created a thing that I can unveil, a sculpture, almost heroic, that I can unveil, which is true. But you? You've come back to the town you were born in, to a girl that won't see you because you put such rot in her body she had to be gutted and hung on a butcher's hook, like a chicken dressed for Sunday. . . . [*He wheels about to strike at her but his raised fist changes its course and strikes down at his own belly and he bends double with a sick cry. Palm Garden wind: whisper of "The Lament."*] Yes, and her brother, who was one of my callers, threatens the same thing for you: castration, if you stay here.

CHANCE: That can't be done to me twice. You did that to me this morning, here on this bed, where I had the honor, where I had the great honor . . .

[*Windy sound rises: They move away from each other, he to the bed, she close to her portable dressing table.*]

PRINCESS: Age does the same thing to a woman. . . . [*Scrapes pearls and pillboxes off table top into handbag.*] Well . . .

[*All at once her power is exhausted, her fury gone. Something uncertain appears in her face and voice betraying the fact which she probably suddenly knows, that her future course is not a progression of triumphs. She still maintains a grand air as she snatches up her platinum mink stole and tosses it about her: it slides immediately off her shoulders; she doesn't seem to notice. He picks the stole up for her, puts it about her shoulders. She grunts disdainfully, her back to him; then resolution falters; she turns to face him with great, dark eyes that are fearful, lonely, and tender.*]

I am going, now, on my way. [*He nods slightly, loosening the Windsor-knot of his knitted black silk tie. Her eyes stay on him.*] Well, are you leaving or staying?

CHANCE: Staying.

PRINCESS: You can't stay here. I'll take you to the next town.

CHANCE: Thanks but no thank you, Princess.

PRINCESS [*seizing his arm*]: Come on, you've got to leave with me. My name is connected with you, we checked in here together. Whatever happens to you, my name will be dragged in with it.

CHANCE: Whatever happens to me's already happened.

PRINCESS: What are you trying to prove?

CHANCE: Something's got to mean something, don't it, Princess? I mean like your life means nothing, except that you never could make it, always almost, never quite? Well, something's still got to mean something.

PRINCESS: I'll send a boy up for my luggage. You'd better come down with my luggage.

CHANCE: I'm not part of your luggage.

PRINCESS: What else can you be?

CHANCE: Nothing . . . but not part of your luggage.

[NOTE: *in this area it is very important that Chance's attitude should be self-recognition but not self-pity—a sort of deathbed dignity and honesty apparent in it. In both Chance and the Princess, we should return to the huddling together of the lost, but not with sentiment, which is false, but with whatever is truthful in the moments when people share doom, face firing squads together. Because the Princess is really equally doomed. She can't turn back the clock any more than can Chance, and the clock is equally relentless to them both. For the Princess: a little, very temporary, return to, recapture of, the spurious glory. The report from Sally Powers may be and probably is a factually accurate report: but to indicate she is going on to further triumph would be to falsify her future. She makes this instinctive admission to herself when she sits down by Chance on the bed, facing the audience. Both are faced with castration, and in her heart she knows it. They sit side by side on the bed like two passengers on a train sharing a bench.*]

PRINCESS: Chance, we've got to go on.

CHANCE: Go on to where? I couldn't go past my youth, but I've gone past it.

[*"The Lament" fades in, continues through the scene to the last curtain.*]

PRINCESS: You're still young, Chance.

CHANCE: Princess, the age of some people can only be calculated by the level of—level of—rot in them. And by that measure I'm ancient.

PRINCESS: What am I?—I know, I'm dead, as old Egypt . . . Isn't it funny? We're still sitting here together, side by side in this room, like we were occupying the same bench on a train—going on together . . . Look. That little donkey's marching around and around to draw water out of a well. . . . [*She points off at something as if outside a train window.*] Look, a shepherd boy's leading a flock.—What an old country, timeless.—Look—

[*The sound of a clock ticking is heard, louder and louder.*]

CHANCE: No, listen. I didn't know there was a clock in this room.

PRINCESS: I guess there's a clock in every room people live in. . . .

CHANCE: It goes tick-tick, it's quieter than your heartbeat, but it's slow dynamite, a gradual explosion, blasting the world we lived in to burnt-out pieces. . . . Time—who could beat it, who could defeat it ever? Maybe some saints and heroes, but not Chance Wayne. I lived on something, that—time?

PRINCESS: Yes, time.

CHANCE: . . . Gnaws away, like a rat gnaws off its own foot caught in a trap, and then, with its foot gnawed off and the rat set free, couldn't run, couldn't go, bled and died. . . .

[*The clock ticking fades away.*]

TOM JUNIOR [*offstage left*]: Miss Del Lago . . .

PRINCESS: I think they're calling our—station. . . .

TOM JUNIOR [*still offstage*]: Miss Del Lago, I have got a driver for you.

[*A trooper enters and waits on gallery. With a sort of tired grace, the Princess rises from the bed, one hand lingering on her seat-companion's shoulder as she moves a little unsteadily to the door. When she opens it, she is confronted by Tom Junior.*]

PRINCESS: Come on, Chance, we're going to change trains at this station. . . . So, come on, we've got to go on. . . . Chance, please. . . .

[*Chance shakes his head and the Princess gives up. She weaves out of sight with the trooper down the corridor. Tom Junior enters from steps, pauses and then gives a low whistle to Scotty, Bud, and third man who enter and stand waiting. Tom Junior comes down bedroom steps and stands on bottom step.*]

CHANCE [*rising and advancing to the forestage*]: I don't ask for your pity, but just for your understanding—not even that—no. Just for your recognition of me in you, and the enemy, time, in us all.

[*The curtain closes.*]

THE END

THE ENEMY: TIME

for George Keathley

CHARACTERS

ROSE
MRS. PITTS
MRS. EBBS
GEORGE
PHIL
MRS. FINLEY
CRIS
PRINCESS PAZMEZOGLU

THE ENEMY: TIME

The play begins with a sound: a sort of wordless lamentation that drifts across the summer night air and dies.

Interior of house lights first: a big grandfather clock with a smiling moon-face dial on a stair landing is lighted and the lamentation fades into the magnified tick of the clock.

The set is skeletal. It includes living room, porch, front walk, and lawn.

Sound: Car radio; car stopping before house.

Rose Finley appears stage left, a short and rather stocky girl of considerable but undistinguished beauty, dressed in black chiffon with black hat and black net gloves: in rather theatrical mourning. Her face wears a look of spirituality and grief, somewhat like a religious painting.

She waits for Phil Beam to appear and they start together toward the house. Phil is a slightly faded Adonis of twenty-nine years: there are lines of anxiety in his almost excessively goodlooking face, his blond hair, somewhat lighter than nature, is receding a bit from its original hairline. He is dressed a little too smartly, in a Hollywood style, wearing a heavy raw silk sport coat in pale blue, a white silk tie with a very light blue silk shirt, matching gold accessories. Before either has spoken, tension is apparent between them.

ROSE [*in an angry whisper*]: Why'd you have to park so far from the house? So you could parade past the porches?

[*A neighbor's voice calls out in a nasal whine.*]

MRS. PITTS: 'S that you Rose?

ROSE: Yes it is, Mrs. Pitts.

MRS. PITTS: Who's that familiar figure I see you with?

ROSE: Don't answer, come on, what're you waiting fo'?

PHIL: See if I've got cigarettes.

ROSE: There's some in the house, come on, before she stops you.

[Phil lingers in pool of light from streetlamp, patting various pockets; Rose stalks furiously ahead to the porch as shadowy female figures appear at edge of light, all in summer housedresses with grey hair untidily loose from pins, their voices drawling in tones of false sweetness, edged with mockery.]

MRS. PITTS: Didn't I tell you that was Phil Beam?

MRS. EBBS: I'll be darned if it ain't!

MRS. PITTS: Hello, stranger.

[Phil has greeted both ladies as he opens a thin gold cigarette case.]

MRS. EBBS [*calling back to man offstage*]: George, it's Phil Beam, George. Come on down here, George, and say hello to Phil. [*Then to Phil.*] He had a slight stroke last winter an' rarely gets off the porch now.

ROSE [*angrily from porch*]: Phil! I'm waiting.

MRS. EBBS: We're not going to hold him long, Rose— Maybe she'll take off that mourning now that you're back in town, Phil.

MRS. PITTS: Nobody knew that she was engaged to that little Connolly boy till he was shot down in the Pacific and become a big war hero: then she put on deep mourning and made it known that they had been secretly engaged since his last homecoming.

ROSE: Phil! I'm going in now!

PHIL: Coming, honey! Hello, George.

[Greets a shuffling man at edge of light.]

GEORGE: 'S that your Cadillac, Phil, or is it rented from one of those Drive Yourself outfits?

PHIL: No. I left my car on the coast, this El Dorado belongs to the Princess Pazmezoglu.

GEORGE: Who in hell's that?

MRS. PITTS: Yes, who's this foreign Princess and what's your connection with her, if I'm not being too nosey?

PHIL: No, you're not being too nosey. Nosiness is natural in old friends. Got a light, George? Ah, thanks. [*Lights his oval gold-tipped cigarette.*] The Princess Pazmezoglu is better known by the name of Dolores De La Costa. You remember Dolores De La Costa, the great star of silent movies? She's now the biggest stockholder in Cosmopolitan, the studio that I've signed with for my next three pictures.

[*They all exclaim with a note of mockery which he seems not to catch.*]

PHIL: Rose is getting impatient, she's heard all this. Evening, friends!

[*He starts toward the porch, a slow, casual saunter, waving a greeting to someone else on a porch.*]

MRS. EBBS: Whatever become of those pictures he talked about making last time he passed through town?

MRS. PITTS: Three years ago, yeah, and before.

GEORGE: [*Laughs evilly.*]

[*The others join his laughter and withdraw into shadow. Phil pauses at edge of steps.*]

PHIL [*glancing back over shoulder*]: Huh? Huh? What's that?

[*They've disappeared. Faint sound of a wordless lamentation in air. A soft light goes on in the parlor. The door is locked.*]

PHIL [*at door*]: Rose?

ROSE [*opening screen door for him*]: You see? No one is deceived, no one is impressed, no one is even interested any more, and yet you do it each time, it's a sort of compulsion with you. It's sad because you did have talent and charm and used to be wonderful looking and a nice boy—once . . .

A couple of times, I guess, you almost made the grade but somehow you always just missed, just barely did miss. Even in our school plays you'd know every line word perfect, and yet on the opening night you'd dry up and have to have the lines hissed at you so loud the audience laughed. But everyone liked you, then. And you deserved it, you were so warm to people, you had that wonderful natural sweetness and warmth toward everyone, Phil, they all loved you. And took it for granted that you would accomplish great things. What happened to you? What was it, Phil? What made you fall out of the sky, such a long way down?

[*She crosses and clings to him a moment. He tries to hold her but she breaks away from him and draws a deep breath and sinks into straight back chair facing audience.*]

[*The wordless lamentation is heard again.*]

PHIL [*as the sound dies out*]: Why do you want to hurt me, now, Rose?

ROSE: Maybe some time I'll tell you. I'm too tired, now.

PHIL: You've needled me all night. Nobody doubts my word in this town but you.

ROSE: Your self-infatuation's become so great you don't see or hear anything but what your vanity wants to . . .

PHIL [*sadly, sweetly*]: Rose, Rose, Rose, Little Rose. . . .

[*He turns sadly to an oval mirror and begins to comb his hair.*]

ROSE: Don't stay any longer, Phil. If you do, I'll say worse things than I've already said.

PHIL: Honey, I know you love me. [*Tenderly to his own image in glass.*] Honey, I know you love me.

ROSE: Are you talking to yourself in the mirror?

PHIL: Now, Rose. . . .

ROSE: How do you know that I love you? By those scratches I gave you when you wouldn't take no for an answer tonight?

PHIL: Yes, by your panicky resistance.

ROSE: I can hear the wires buzzing tomorrow all over town, Rose Finley and Phil Beam arrested on Lovers Lane for indecent behavior in a parked car. Nobody will believe that I fought like a tiger to get out of the car, unless they publish a photo of those scratches.

PHIL: Try to stick to facts. Will you try to stick to the facts? It was not Lovers Lane and nobody got arrested.

ROSE: Flashlight turned on us, insulted and told to drive off.

PHIL: You brought it on by starting that commotion.

ROSE: Defending myself from your attempts to attack me?

PHIL: Attack you, honey? Me? Phil Beam? I've never lifted a finger in my life to get anybody's love. I've had the opposite problem, avoiding love with them. Too much of my energy's been dissipated that way, giving myself to people that made emotional demands on me because I was kind, understanding, and . . .

ROSE: Finish the sentence. And what? Beautiful? Don't remove those gold hairs caught in the comb. Put them away, save them. Enclose one hair in each letter to your fans when you answer your fan-mail with a—glamorous photo signed, Sincerely, Phil Beam, or Prince Pazmezoglu or the—Blond Liberace . . . What is it, Mother?

[*A petulant voice has called 'Rose' upstairs.*]

MRS. FINLEY: Who're you with down there?

ROSE: I'm saying goodnight to Phil Beam.

MRS. FINLEY: Oh! Well, hurry!

[*Door slams above.*]

PHIL [*wounded*]: Not 'Hello, Phil, how are you?' Just 'Oh, well, hurry!' What's come over the people in this town? What is it? I don't understand what's happened!

ROSE: Mama says you're corrupt.

PHIL: She says I'm what?

ROSE: You heard me.

PHIL: Corrupt? That's not a word that's used lightly. When did she say that about me? What provoked such a statement? I think I ought to explain the libel laws to your mother. She seems to be ignorant of the libel laws in this country. Nobody with any self-respect permits himself to be called corrupt. And my self-respect has not suffered. My feelings, yes, but my self-respect, no. I think I will have to ask Mrs. Finley for some explanation of the use of that word to—

[*He starts up the stairs to the landing.*]

ROSE: I wouldn't if I were you.

PHIL: But you're not me! Mrs. Finley? Oh, Mrs. Finley!

[*The call is not loud and there is no response to it. The sound of the clock is brought up. He turns to the grinning moon-face on the dial of the grandfather clock. The wordless lamentation in the air . . .*]

PHIL: You know, the big enemy's time? Time's the big enemy. Rose . . .

[*Turns from clock: but stays on landing in soft light.*]

Not any foreign power, just time. The one big enemy of everything that exists!—the source of corruption . . .

ROSE: Yes.

PHIL: And yet they make these enormous clocks for houses, clocks as tall as a man or half a head taller and put them on the stair-landing so they look down over the living-room of the house and say, "tick-tick, you're dying. . . ." Not shouting, not raising a rumpus, just saying, "tick-tick, you're dying" yes, in a whisper, like some bitchy, gossipy old lady, "tick, tick, tick, tick, tick, tick," just tick, one syllable for one second that won't come again, and that's more important than anything anyone human can say or think of. Slow dynamite! A gradual-explosion!—blasting the whole universe to—rotten—pieces. . . .

[*This has been a sort of interior monologue; he comes down the stairs.*]

I'll call Mrs. Finley, your mother, up in the morning and ask her what she meant when she called me corrupt. . . .

[*He opens screen door.*]

I'm goin' outside, I feel sick. . . .

ROSE: I don't know what's happened to me. I guess I've had everything, and don't like it anymore. I've had it all, all of it, and now I know I don't like it. I'm not even sure I'm wearing mourning for him. . . .

[*This is also an interior monologue: She picks up the dead hero's picture.*]

Perhaps it's for me, for my youth, for the life removed from my body when I was—sick.

[*Sets picture down sadly.*]

But it's all lost its meaning, or taste, yes, like a thing that you eat but don't have any more taste for, that's turned to saw-dust in your mouth. . . .

[*Her hands touch her breasts as if she had a pain there. She sighs and reaches under black chiffon: Loosens brassiere and removes it, stuffing it under pillow of sofa. Then she goes out on the porch.*]

I think I'll go in a convent.

PHIL: What did you say then, Rose?

ROSE: I said I thought that I would go into a convent.

PHIL: Oh. [*Grins harshly.*]

ROSE: Don't laugh, Phil. I mean it.

PHIL: Is that why you took off your bra? And came out here with your bosom exposed to the moonlight through that gauze?

ROSE: The strap's been cutting all night. I turned off the porch light and no one can see me but you and we're like brother and sister, now, to each other. . . .

[*She means this. He stares at at her with his tight smile, his hands clenched.*]

On that basis, we can talk to each other and offer each other advice.

PHIL: Helpful advice starts with truth. Let's be truthful. It wasn't because the strap of your bra was too tight that you took it off. It was—maybe unconscious!—but an act of cruelty, for revenge! Nothing's more cruel than rousing desire in a man and saying "No!" to him . . . When you did it in the parked car, that was forgivable, you had to get back at me, once, for going away so often and leaving you stuck here! But this is a little too much, this is—too much!

[*He seizes her shoulders.*]

ROSE: Phil.

PHIL: Take me in the house, baby.

ROSE: No, Phil.

PHIL: Jesus, just let me touch you, just let me hold you a second.

ROSE: I honestly didn't think that . . . !

[*Wrests herself violently free and rushes inside screen door. He starts to enter. She latches the screen. He falls back panting. The worldless chant of mourning is repeated in the night air.*]

Phil? Phil? My body doesn't exist for me anymore. Do you want to know why? Shall I tell you? Through this screendoor, or would you rather go back to the Princess Pazmezoglu at the hotel without knowing?

PHIL: Knowing what?

ROSE: You remember the last time you were in town? Let's see, it was five years ago, in late summer. . . . You were stone broke. I stole money from Mama so you could buy your bus ticket to New York where you were so sure of getting the lead in some big musical that you didn't even get a job in the chorus. But disappeared so completely that when I wrote you care of Actors' Equity like you'd told me, the letter came back stamped "Unknown"!

PHIL: No. I haven't forgotten any part of all the long and desperate struggle I made before my luck turned at last.

ROSE: Well, I'm not talking about your struggle. I am talking about the last time you came home and we resumed our relations. Well, when you left I was—

PHIL: What?

ROSE: Sick.

PHIL: You mean you—?

ROSE: I mean I was sick! Sick! S-I-C-K! Sick!

[*She faces him fiercely through screen.*]

Now go away! I've told you! If you somehow didn't know it before, you know now!

PHIL [*hoarsely*]: Rose? Rose, darling? Rose?

ROSE [*in a fierce whisper*]: I didn't know what it was, I'd never even heard of it till I got it from you, you rotten phoney.

PHIL: What, Rose? What, for God's sake, what, what!?

ROSE: A social disease: that's called by a 4 letter word!

PHIL: —Aw, God, I——didn't know, Rose!

ROSE: How could you not know and have it? And give it to me?! I asked the doctor if it was possible for a man to not know and have it. He said it's unmistakable in a man and even an innocent boy would know the symptoms.

PHIL: Honey, I had a slight, slight little touch of it weeks before the last time I was in town but I took treatment and it was over, I swear. Later it—showed up again, but—that was a long time after. . . .

[*Stares at her desperately through screen.*]

Jesus, no wonder you won't let me touch you now!

[*Begins suddenly to sob: Leaning his face against screen. After a few moments she unlatches the screen and pushes him gently aside so she can come out on the porch.*]

ROSE: Now Phil. That's enough. It's all, all over with now.

[*She tosses her cigarette onto lawn.*]

Phil, stop crying, now, Phil. I don't feel any hatred, I don't feel any malice, not even any resentment, I just feel—pity for you. . . .

[*She sits on wicker chair and takes another cigarette from his case.*]

Unfortunately for me, because of my ignorance of such special matters, I took too long in discovering what had happened, a thing as incredible as being infected with a social disease by a boy who'd been my lover since I was fourteen. . . .

[*Leans back in chair.*]

A boy that I'd idolized and adored for ten years despite all—gossip about him. . . .

[*Turns her face to him again.*]

Shall I tell you the end of this ugly little story?

[*Lamentation in air.*]

I guess I might as well tell you all of it now. Being so ignorant, not knowing what was the matter, I let it go on too long. The life-bearing part of my body was so diseased that it had to be cut out. . . .

[*She descends steps into lawn. He stays in the moonvine shadows on the porch.*]

So now you see I am all cold and pure inside, yes, dead as that dead planet that goes round and round like the hand of a clock keeping time. . . .

[*The worldless chant of lamentation.*]

Love is so far from me now that—I wasn't even conscious of exposing my breasts to you when I took off my brassiere! [*Throws back her head in quiet, desperate laughter.*] I wear black for—what? Not the boy that I said that I was engaged to when he died. . . . For us, you and me, Phil Beam!! And our youth that died by the slow tick tick of the clock. . . . The slow tick tick of corruption. . . .

[*Car draws up before house. And Rose's brother strides on-stage, a boy of nineteen, swaying a bit from liquor, sullen-faced, menacing.*]

PHIL: Hi, Cris.

CRIS: I heard you were here with my sister.

PHIL: News travels fast in this—

CRIS: Go in, Rose. I wanta talk alone to him.

ROSE: Cris, you're full of liquor. Go up to bed.

CRIS: [*Turning fiercely to Phil.*] You took my sister out on Tiger Tail Road tonight and parked in a dark place and tried to corrupt her again and the state patrol stopped you?

ROSE: That's not what happened. Cris, go up to bed, please.

CRIS: Don't tell me what didn't happen, I know what happened, and it's going to be in the papers. And he's going to be in the jail.

PHIL: Cris, you know me better.

CRIS: Hell, I know you too well. Come on down in the basement and let's have it out!

ROSE: Cris! Go to bed!

CRIS [*to her*]: I'm not as crazy about bed-going as you are. You go to bed, alone, and leave me here with this bastard!

PHIL: Now, Cris, this is awf'ly silly! Cant you see it's silly?

CRIS: Laugh, phoney, you'll be laughing on the other side of your face! Who do you think you're fooling with that tacky Cadillac, with the long silver horns you got parked in front of this house? Who's it belong to, huh? Hell, not you! Let me see the car registration for it. Huh? Let me see the goddam registration before I. . . .

PHIL: [*Opens gold cigarette case with air of tolerant boredom.*]

CRIS: Come on down to the basement.

ROSE: Cris, if you don't go in I'm going to call Mother. People are still on porches all over this block!

CRIS: I don't give a—

PHIL: Cris? Cris? You're my girl's young brother. Your sister and I went steady in this town when you were peddling papers on Walgreen's corner. Remember? And summer evenings when you were cutting the lawn, I'd come by and say, 'Let me cut it for you' and I would hand you a buck and lend you my second-hand Chevy to ride around town in with the coon tails flying! Tooling down Front Street blowing those three-noted horns . . . Have you forgotten this quick?

CRIS: Not a thing!—Phoney!—And all that time you was out corrupting my sister!

ROSE: Cris: I'm going to call Mother.

[*Tense pause. Lamentation in air.*]

CRIS: Father O'Malley wants you to call him up, Rose. He says he wants you to see him now, tonight. He's talked to the editor of the paper, in fact him and me both did, and your name won't be mentioned in the story.

PHIL: What story?

CRIS: The article about your arrest on Tiger Tail for trying to corrupt my sister again in a parked borrowed car. Or one stolen.

PHIL: I wasn't arrested. Nobody was arrested. Your sister and I were visiting our old hangouts and talking about old times. A cop drove up and turned a flashlight on us and asked to look at my papers. I showed him my papers. He said excuse me and left. That's the whole story.

CRIS: Then why did I hear about it? Come on down in the basement.

PHIL: I'll go down in the basement, but Cris—

CRIS: Just come down in the basement round the back way so we won't wake up Mom!

PHIL: I've never fought with anyone in my life.

CRIS: That's for sure.

PHIL: But I'm not afraid to go in the basement with you.

CRIS: Then what're you holding back for?

PHIL: I'm not holding back.

CRIS: Come on!—Then. Big Deal! Pretty boy! Phoney!

[*They go round the side of house. The night seems very peaceful with locusts singing in the late summer trees. Rose sits very still with eyes closed but hands clenched tight on the wicker chair arms. There comes a muffled cry from the basement. She catches her breath in a loud gasp and half rises but sinks back again. The muffled out-cry is repeated. She half rises again and falls back and covers her face. Sound of a cab driving up before house. Door of cab opens and a woman's voice with a foreign accent is heard.*]

VOICE: Wait.

[*A large heavy woman appears: She is best described as a very rich old Gypsy whose dress is a bizarre compromise between the Orient, or Levantine, and the West. Gems glitter wherever they can. Her eyelids are painted blue. Despite the hot night, she wears a silver mink stole and her black slippers have big rhinestone buckles.*]

How do you do, young lady. I am Phil Beam's employer and I am looking for him and I was told he was here. And I see my Cadillac in front of this house.

ROSE: Phil is here.

PRINCESS: Where? I don't see him.

ROSE: He'll be out soon. Would you like to sit down?

PRINCESS: Has he gone to the powder room?

ROSE: No, he's in the basement.

PRINCESS: In the basement? What for!

ROSE: My brother is having a conversation with him.

PRINCESS: Oh. Is that the disturbance?

ROSE: Yes, I'm afraid so.

PRINCESS: You should have stopped it, my dear.

ROSE: I tried to. But maybe it's justice.

PRINCESS: You shouldn't have let this happen. Phil requires severe treatment sometimes, but beating him up is no good. Life has done that to him lots of times and will do it continually from now till he dies a cheap death. Do you know who I am?

ROSE: You're Princess Pazmezoglu and you used to be a silent film star. You quit movies when the talkies came in.

PRINCESS: I'm going to sit down. Yes. I did retire. Because of my accent, but not until after I'd made a couple of million that's well-invested. I found Phil Beam on a beach in Florida. He was rubbing oil in the bodies of fat millionaires. I was one of the bodies that he rubbed the oil into. [*Laughs sadly.*] He did this well, I employed him. He'll have a future with me as long as he toes the line, but he's got to toe it. I don't put up with nonsense. I know the power of money. I have that power. I think the disturbance is over. . . .

[*Phil comes around the side of the house, unsteadily, badly beaten.*]

Well, Phil. Have you learned anything about the mistakes of homecoming?

PHIL: [*Gives her a brief, sick look: then looks at the sky with clenched hands held before him and then hurls his body onto the ground and twists and writhes there.*]

ROSE: Excuse me. I'm going in now. Try to understand him; I never could.

[*She enters the house. Pause. Locusts sing.)*

PRINCESS: Phil? Phil! There's people on porches up and down the block looking at you, you know. I'm going to drive back to the hotel in my car. . . . [*She crosses out of sight, serenely, perhaps somewhat pleased. To Cabbie.*] What do I owe you? Oh. Here is a dollar.

[*Taxi drives off. Slight pause. A car door slams and we hear the rich, smooth sound of a luxury car driving off. Phil makes another brief convulsive move on the lawn: Then rolls on his back, arms flung out and looks up at the sky. The lights in the house go out. The lamentation in the air rises again. Phil draws himself up to his feet, his face bloody, and addresses the night sky.*]

PHIL: What is it? Oh, God, what is it! I don't understand what it is. . . .

CURTAIN

Hart Crane's line, "Relentless caper for all those who step The legend of their youth into the noon," serves as a symbolic epigraph to *Sweet Bird of Youth*, in which the characters try to carry their youth into the "noon" of their lives. Quickly flying by the windows at the Royal Palms Hotel while musical strains of "The Lament" are heard in the background, the sweet bird of youth appears to each character and then disappears, never to return.

Once a goddess of the silver screen, Andrea Del Lago is now past her prime seeking pleasure in alcohol, drugs, and young studs whom she dominates, leading them around like lapdogs bound to her by an invisible chain. Wheezing for her oxygen and squinting through her broken glasses, she searches for her Moroccan hashish while ordering her current young stud, Chance Wayne, about as if he were her slave. A sort of lament drifts through the air as the Princess observes it seems to be saying "Lost, lost, never to be found again." In his "Foreword" to *Sweet Bird of Youth*, Williams observes, "We are all civilized people, which means we are all savages at heart but observing a few amenities of civilized behavior." Princess recognizes the savage monster in herself, "the flesh-hungry, blood thirsty ogre" at the top of the beanstalk lost in the beanstalk country," exclaiming to Chance, "When monster meets monster, one monster has to give way, AND IT WILL NEVER BE ME. I'm an older hand at it . . . with much more aptitude at it than you have . . ." In the final scene after she drearns of her "come back" as an aging actress with talent, she is aware of the fleeting nature of such "success" and encourages Chance to join her: "I've climbed back alone up the beanstalk to the ogre's country where I live, now, alone . . . Chance, we've got to go on."

What once was, no longer is. Chance's girl Heavenly is no longer fifteen, innocent, uncorrupted, and pure. Having presumably contracted venereal disease from Chance during one of his return visits to St. Cloud, she suffered a hysterectomy and, as her father crudely observes, was "spayed like a dawg." Her father, who could have saved her by letting her marry, as she says, "a boy that was still young and clean," exploited her by trying to pressure her into marrying "a fifty-year old money bag" from whom he wanted something. This scenario of abuse was repeated over and over. Feeling "dead, cold, empty, like an old woman," Heavenly explains to her father, "I feel as if I ought to rattle like a dead dried up vine when the Gulf Wind blows"—a description that is echoed by the Princess when she says "What am I? I know, I'm dead, as old as Egypt . . ."

Even Boss Finley has experienced the passing of the sweet bird of youth—his daughter observes that he married for love, but that he wouldn't allow his daughter to do the same. At one point when he looks at his lovely daughter Heavenly, Boss Finley's reveries carry him back to a time of youth and innocence, his own. Williams tells us in the stage directions: "It's important not to think of his attitude toward her in terms of crudely conscious incestuous feeling, but just in the natural terms of almost any aging father's feeling for a beautiful young daughter who reminds him of a dead wife that he desired intensely when she was the age of his daughter." Now his mistress Miss Lucy represents the lie that he has been living. While thriving on Finley's money, she mocks the old man by writing on the walls of the ladies' room at the Royal Palms Hotel: "Boss Finley, . . . is too old to cut the mustard." Could there have really been an idyllic time past, as he explains in his "populist messiah" campaign speech, when he came "down barefoot out of the red clay hills as if the Voice of God called" him.

In spite of the names St. Cloud and Diamond Key, a grand hotel, a grove of royal palm trees, and a stage design that opens up under a star-lit sky, the world of *Sweet Bird of Youth* is a spiritual wasteland, the ogre's country at the top of the beanstalk, a land sold to the power brokers of oil interests, a "city of flames" where the "unsatisfied tiger" rages "in the nerves jungle," a place where the "Voice of God" has long been gone. "Lost, Lost," Princess explains, we are all living in "places of exile from whatever we loved." Perhaps the Heckler has the answer when he shouts, "I believe that the silence of God, the absolute speechlessness of Him is a long, long and awful thing that the whole world is lost because of." In the world of St. Cloud, God is apparently dead.

In this savage land of culprits and victims, predators and preyed upon, and those who are bought and those who do the buying, the "American Dream," like God, is a long time gone. Ironically, its spirit echoes throughout *Sweet Bird of Youth*. Chance Wayne sets forth from St. Cloud believing in optimism, self-reliance, and self-sufficiency; that his is a land of infinite possibilities; that it is possible to rise from rags to riches; and that individual merit and worth are valued. He has a dream that he will not relinquish under any circumstances. Boss Finley begins his political career as "a man with a mission, which he holds sacred, and on the strength of which he rises to high public office." Greed, pride, selfishness, opportunism, cynicism, being "Number One," finding the easy way to wealth, asking "What's in it for me?" have brought about the rise of ogres and monsters in beanstalk country. American has become the beanstalk country.

Political rhetoric runs throughout the world of Tennessee Williams. Sometimes it is partially disguised; at other times, direct and powerful. Ideas involving political power brokers and ruthless industrialists dominate the atmosphere of *Sweet Bird of Youth*. Boss Finley is the predator politician, but he is, ironically, also the prey of forces more powerful than he, such as his state's governor and the corporate oil barons. According to Joseph Heller in *Catch-22*, "Every culprit is a victim; and every victim, a culprit." Orwell's Big Brother, Heller's Milo Minderbinder, and Williams' own Syndicate in *Baby Doll*, the Klan in *Orpheus Descending*, Gutman and Generalissimo in *Camino Real*, and Red Devil Battery operatives in *The Red Devil Battery Sign*, show the individual to be powerless in the face of forces too big and overwhelming to be taken in battle. To entice Heavenly to join his campaign willingly, Boss Finley tries to coax her into going to New Orleans on a spending spree, explaining, "I made a pile of dough on a deal involvin' the sale of rights to oil under water here lately." He thinks he is the one doing the buying; but, in another turn of irony, he is the one who has been bought. Young Tom Finley has turned his young supporters for his father's candidacy for office into a gang of juvenile delinquents, capable of beating hecklers into silence and castrating a black man in a display of their fragile and corrupt power. Echoes of Heller's omnipresent "mobs with clubs" in his surreal depiction of the Eternal City of Rome in *Catch-22* ("Hell") appear throughout the political action of *Sweet Bird of Youth*. Shakespeare's power broker Bolingbroke in Richard I, Robert Penn Warren's "just a country boy" Willie Stark in *All the King's Men*, Huey P. Long (Machiavellian governor of Louisiana), and Orval Faubus (governor of Arkansas who opposed segregation) might be considered proper analogues to Boss Finley. His name is "Legion."

The genius of Williams involves his use of classical allusions, Biblical stories, mythic archtypes, fairy tales and legends, and historical analogies from the past and present in his plays. He almost always twists, even inverts them, challenging us to discover the ironic and often grotesque transformations of the originals. Is Andrea Del Lago's "Sleeping Beauty" brought to life by a gigolo carrying a canister of oxygen? Who is Jack, who is the ogre, what beanstalk is Jack trying to climb, and what treasure is he trying to steal?

Williams observes the unities of time, place, and action in *Sweet Bird of Youth* as the onstage course of events occur on Easter Sunday, from late morning until late night. This sharpens the focus of the conflict significantly. References made to Good Friday expand the religious dimensions of the play. How might this be considered a story of death, resurrection and salvation? How is the passion of Christ distorted in this dramatic analogue?

Trying to dominate the disturbance in the hall at his political rally in St. Cloud, Boss Finley proclaims: "Last Friday, Good Friday, I seen a horrible thing on the campus of our great State

University, which I built for the State. A hideous straw-stuffed effigy of myself, Tom Finley, was hung and set fire to in the main quadrangle of the college." He goes on to explain, "This outrage was inspired . . . inspired by the Northern radical press. However, that was Good Friday. Today is Easter. I saw that was Good Friday. Today is Easter Sunday and I am in St. Cloud." This takes place simultaneously with the overwhelming and systematic beating of the Heckler. This is not the resurrection of his political career dreamed of by Boss Finley.

Chance Wayne is also attempting a resurrection of sorts. This is his last chance to recapture the heart of Heavenly; defeat the keepers of her southern, "virgin," white persona; and carry her off to Hollywood to co-star with him in a movie to be called "Youth." He rides into town driving the Cadillac convertible of a movie star, has his name paged continuously at the Royal Palms Hotel, flaunts his movie contract, and declares a new day dawning. Brought to face the reality that he is past his youth, the corrupter of his girl, filled with rot, and the victim of time, he accepts the cards has been dealt. When Princess warns him that he is to be castrated if he does not leave with her, he tells her, "That can't be done to me twice. You did that to me this morning, here on this bed, where I had the honor, where I had the great honor . . . ." Might this be considered a sort of crucifixion, one without a resurrection? Chance is unable to prove anything through his suffering and "death." He questions, "Something's got to mean something, don't it, Princess? I mean like your life means nothing, except that you never could make it, always almost, never quite? Well, something's got to mean something." The story has been drastically changed to one involving defeat and tragedy rather than rebirth and resurrection.

In a final turnabout, Chance is savior to Alexandra Del Lago. There is a resurrection in *Sweet Bird of Youth* that goes significantly beyond her comeback as a movie star with creative talent. Born again, she enthusiastically exclaims to Chance, "Chance, the most wonderful thing has happened to me . . . Chance, when I saw you driving under the window with your head held high, with that terrible stiff-necked pride of the defeated which I know so well; I knew that your come-back had been a failure like mine. And I felt something in my heart for you." Feeling something for someone other than herself, she goes on, "That means my heart's still alive, at least some part of it is, not all of my heart is dead yet. Part's still alive. . . . Chance, gave me hope that I could stop being a monster. . . . You gave oxygen to me." Instead of being a monster in beanstalk country, perhaps she has become a unique "lady of the lake," one who has dared to see her self-reflection in its glassy waters, accept it for what it is, and "go on" to a new reality that awaits her.

COLBY H. KULLMAN
THE UNIVERSITY OF MISSISSIPPI

A CHRONOLOGY

1907 June 3: Cornelius Coffin Williams and Edwina Estelle Dakin marry in Columbus, Mississippi.

1909 November 19: Sister, Rose Isabelle Williams, is born in Columbus, Mississippi.

1911 March 26: Thomas Lanier Williams III is born in Columbus, Mississippi.

1918 July: Williams family moves to St. Louis, Missouri.

1919 February 21: Brother, Walter Dakin Williams, is born in St. Louis, Missouri.

1928 Short story "The Vengeance of Nitocris" is published in *Weird Tales* magazine.

July: Williams' grandfather, Walter Edwin Dakin (1857-1954), takes young Tom on a tour of Europe.

1929 September: Begins classes at the University of Missouri at Columbia.

1930 Writes the one-act play *Beauty is the Word* for a local contest.

1932 Summer: Fails ROTC and is taken out of college by his father and put to work as a clerk at the International Shoe Company.

1936 January: Enrolls in extension courses at Washington University, St. Louis.

1937 March 18 and 20: First full-length play, *Candles to the Sun*, is produced by the Mummers, a semi-professional theater company in St. Louis.

September: Transfers to the University of Iowa.

November 30 and December 4: *Fugitive Kind* is performed by the Mummers.

1938 Graduates from the University of Iowa with a degree in English.

Completes the play, *Not About Nightingales.*

1939 *Story* magazine publishes "The Field of Blue Children" with the first printed use of his professional name, "Tennessee Williams."

Receives an award from the Group Theatre for a group of short plays collectively titled *American Blues*, which leads to his association with Audrey Wood, his agent for the next thirty-two years.

1940 January through June: Studies playwriting with John Gassner at the New School for Social Research in New York City.

December 30: *Battle of Angels*, starring Miriam Hopkins, suffers a disastrous first night during its out-of-town try-out in Boston and closes shortly thereafter.

1942 December: At a cocktail party thrown by Lincoln Kirstein in New York, meets James Laughlin, founder of New Directions, who is to become Williams' lifelong friend and publisher.

1943 Drafts a screenplay, *The Gentleman Caller*, while under contract in Hollywood with Metro Goldwyn Mayer: rejected by the studio, he later rewrites it as *The Glass Menagerie.*

October 13: A collaboration with his friend Donald Windham, *You Touched Me!* (based on a story by D.H. Lawrence), premieres at the Cleveland Playhouse.

1944 December 26: *The Glass Menagerie* opens in Chicago starring Laurette Taylor.

A group of poems titled "The Summer Belvedere" is published in *Five Young American Poets, 1944.* (All books listed here are published by New Directions unless otherwise indicated.)

1945 March 25: *Stairs to the Roof* premieres at the Pasadena Playhouse in California.

March 31: *The Glass Menagerie* opens on Broadway and goes on to win the Drama Critics Circle Award for best play of the year.

September 25: *You Touched Me!* opens on Broadway, and is later published by Samuel French.

December: 27 Wagons Full of Cotton and Other Plays is published.

1947 Summer: Meets Frank Merlo (1929-1963) in Provincetown—starting in 1948 they become lovers and companions, and remain together for fourteen years.

December 3: *A Streetcar Named Desire,* directed by Elia Kazan and starring Jessica Tandy, Marlon Brando, Kim Hunter and Karl Malden, opens on Broadway to rave reviews and wins the Pulitzer Prize and the Drama Critics Circle Award.

1948 October 6: *Summer and Smoke* opens on Broadway and closes in just over three months.

1949 January: *One Arm and Other Stories* is published.

1950 The novel *The Roman Spring of Mrs. Stone* is published.

The film version of *The Glass Menagerie* is released.

1951 February 3: *The Rose Tattoo* opens on Broadway starring Maureen Stapleton and Eli Wallach and wins the Tony Award for best play of the year.

The film version of *A Streetcar Named Desire* is released starring Vivian Leigh as Blanche and Marlon Brando as Stanley.

1952 April 24: A revival of *Summer and Smoke* directed by Jose Quintero and starring Geraldine Page opens off-Broadway at the Circle at the Square and is a critical success.

The National Institute of Arts and Letters inducts Williams as a member.

1953 March 19: *Camino Real* opens on Broadway and after a harsh critical reception closes within two months.

1954 A book of stories, *Hard Candy*, is published in August.

1955 March 24: *Cat on a Hot Tin Roof* opens on Broadway directed by Elia Kazan and starring Barbara Bel Geddes, Ben Gazzara and Burl Ives. *Cat* wins the Pulitzer Prize and the Drama Critics Circle Award.

The film version of *The Rose Tattoo*, for which Anna Magnani later wins an Academy Award, is released.

1956 The film *Baby Doll*, with a screenplay by Williams and directed by Elia Kazan, is released amid some controversy and is blacklisted by Catholic leader Cardinal Spellman.

June: *In the Winter of Cities*, Williams' first book of poetry, is published.

1957 March 21: *Orpheus Descending*, a revised version of *Battle of Angels*, directed by Harold Clurman, opens on Broadway but closes after two months.

1958 February 7: *Suddenly Last Summer* and *Something Unspoken* open off-Broadway under the collective title *Garden District*.

The film version of *Cat on a Hot Tin Roof* is released.

1959 March 10: *Sweet Bird of Youth* opens on Broadway and runs for three months.

The film version of *Suddenly Last Summer*, with a screenplay by Gore Vidal, is released.

1960 November 10: The comedy *Period of Adjustment* opens on Broadway and runs for over four months.

The film version of *Orpheus Descending* is released under the title *The Fugitive Kind*.

1961 December 29: *The Night of the Iguana* opens on Broadway and runs for nearly ten months.

The film versions of *Summer and Smoke* and *The Roman Spring of Mrs. Stone* are released.

1962 The film versions of *Sweet Bird of Youth* and *Period of Adjustment* are released.

1963 January 15: *The Milk Train Doesn't Stop Here Anymore* opens on Broadway and closes immediately due to a blizzard and a newspaper strike. It is revived January 1, 1964 in a Broadway production starring Tallulah Bankhead and Tab Hunter and closes within a week.

September: Frank Merlo dies of lung cancer.

1964 The film version of *Night of the Iguana* is released.

1966 February 22: *Slapstick Tragedy* (*The Mutilated* and *The Gnädiges Fräulein*) runs on Broadway for less than a week.

December: A novella and stories are published under the title *The Knightly Quest*.

1968 March 27: *Kingdom of Earth* opens on Broadway under the title *The Seven Descents of Myrtle*.

The film version of *The Milk Train Doesn't Stop Here Anymore* is released under the title *Boom*!

1969 May 11: *In the Bar of a Tokyo Hotel* opens off-Broadway and runs for three weeks.

Committed by his brother Dakin for three months to the Renard Psychiatric Division of Barnes Hospital in St. Louis.

The film version of *Kingdom of Earth* is released under the title *The Last of the Mobile Hot Shots*.

Awarded Doctor of Humanities degree by the University of Missouri and a Gold Medal for Drama by the American Academy of Arts and Letters.

1970 February: A book of plays, *Dragon Country*, is published.

1971 Williams breaks with his agent Audrey Wood. Bill Barnes assumes his representation, and then later Mitch Douglas.

1972 April 2: *Small Craft Warnings* opens off-Broadway.

Williams is given a Doctor of Humanities degree by the University of Hartford.

1973 March 1: *Out Cry*, the revised version of *The Two-Character Play*, opens on Broadway.

1974 September: *Eight Mortal Ladies Possessed*, a book of short stories, is published.

Williams is presented with an Entertainment Hall of Fame Award and a Medal of Honor for Literature from the National Arts Club.

1975 The novel *Moise and the World of Reason* is published by Simon and Schuster and Williams' *Memoirs* is published by Doubleday.

1976 January 20: *This Is (An Entertainment)* opens in San Francisco at the American Conservatory Theater.

June: *The Red Devil Battery Sign* closes during its out-of-town tryout in Boston.

November 23: *Eccentricities of a Nightingale*, a rewritten version of *Summer and Smoke*, opens in New York.

April: Williams' second volume of poetry, *Androgyne, Mon Amour*, is published.

1977 May 11: *Vieux Carrè* opens on Broadway and closes within two weeks.

1978 *Tiger Tail* premieres at the Alliance Theater in Atlanta, Georgia and a revised version premieres the following year at the Hippodrome Theater in Gainsville, Florida.

1979 January 10: *A Lovely Sunday for Creve Coeur* opens off-Broadway.

Kirche, Küche, Kinder premieres off-Broadway at the Jean Cocteau Repertory Theater.

Williams is presented with a Lifetime Achievement Award at the Kennedy Center Honors in Washington by President Jimmy Carter.

1980 January 25: *Will Mr. Merriwether Return from Memphis?* premieres for a limited run at the Tennessee Williams Performing Arts Center in Key West, Florida.

March 26: Williams' last Broadway play, *Clothes for a Summer Hotel*, opens and closes after 15 performances.

1981 August 24: *Something Cloudy, Something Clear* premieres off-Broadway at the Jean Cocteau Repertory Theater.

1982 May 8: The second of two versions of *A House Not Meant to Stand* opens for a limited run at the Goodman Theater in Chicago.

1983 February 24: Williams is found dead in his room at the Hotel Elysee in New York City. It is determined from an autopsy that the playwright died from asphyxiation, choking on a plastic medicine cap. Williams is later buried in St. Louis.

1984 July: *Stopped Rocking and Other Screenplays* is published.

1985 November: *Collected Stories*, with an introduction by Gore Vidal, is published.

1995 The first half of Lyle Leverich's important biography, *Tom: The Unknown Tennessee Williams* is published by Crown Publishers.

1996 September 5: Rose Isabelle Williams dies in Tarrytown, New York.

September 5: *The Notebook of Trigorin*, in a version

revised by Williams, opens at the Cincinnati Playhouse in the Park.

1998 March 5: *Not About Nightingales* premieres at the Royal National Theatre in London, directed by Trevor Nunn, later moves to Houston, Texas, and opens November 25, 1999 on Broadway.

1999 November: *Spring Storm* is published.

2000 May: *Stairs to the Roof* is published.

November: *The Selected Letters of Tennessee Williams, Volume I* is published.

2001 June: *Fugitive Kind* is published.

2002 April: *Collected Poems* is published.

2004 August: *Candles to the Sun* is published.

November: *The Selected Letters of Tennessee Williams, Volume II* is published.

2005 April: *Mister Paradise and Other One-Act Plays* is published.

2008 April: *A House Not Meant to Stand* and *The Traveling Companion and Other Plays* are published.

May 20: Walter Dakin Williams dies at the age of 89 in Belleville, Illinois.